"I think it's great when stories are dark
and strange and weirdly personal."

-- Robin Williams

Perk at Work books by Jason Salas

Perk at Work Vol. 1: "Open for Business"
Perk at Work Vol. 2: "Another Day, Another Dollar"

A **PerkATWork** book

Fine Line, LLC, New Mexico

Perk at Work is a comic strip about a café worker, Perk, and his interactions with his boss, his cook, and his regular customers.

The café is located on the ground floor of a downtown multi-story office building. Mr. Argyle owns the building and the café. Workers from the varied businesses in and around the building patronize the café when they need to grab a bite to eat, take a coffee break, or simply just want to step away from the desk and hang out.

So when you're getting a little burnt out and the corners of your mouth need a lift, visit *Perk at Work*. He'll get the job done!

www.perkatworkcomic.com

Coffee Break Stories
The first four short stories featuring the characters from the comic strip *Perk at Work.*

ISBN 978-0-9894489-1-8
© 2015 Jason Salas

Fine Line, LLC
PO Box 901
Las Cruces, NM 88004

Printed in the United States of America

Contents

Introductions
Are
In
Order

Sometimes you search for your jobs. Sometimes they come to you. And other times, rare times, it's a bit of both.

It's Monday morning, 6:25 AM. The spring air is crisp but not cold. Downtown is quiet but there is some life starting to bubble up.

In the corner of an office building is a café. The sign on the door says it's open but nobody is dining. Perk cups his hand to the window to shade the glare. Behind the counter is a ragged-looking Hispanic man wearing a short-order cook's hat. He is eying his reflection in a spoon. Perk enters the café, newspaper in hand, and surveys his surroundings. The café is small and nondescript. There are amateurish southwest style paintings peppering the walls. No music plays. The door closes behind Perk and the ragged man looks up from the spoon.

"So you're the guy?" the cook asks in accented English.

"I'm sorry?" Perk replies.

"You should be. You're late. You were supposed to be here at six. You're lucky I didn't call Boss Man. And where's your shirt? Didn't they give you a polo?"

"I'm sorry?"

"Don't sweat it. Just get one out of the box in back!" The cook looks back at his reflection and points in the general area of the kitchen. "And hurry up. I don't want anyone to come in before you're ready. I don't like dealing with the peoples."

"I'm here about the job." Perk holds up the newspaper.

"Duh." As warned, the cook is obviously not a people person.

Perk takes a couple of steps toward the kitchen and stops. "Are you saying I should start right now?"

"What part of *'Duh'* don't you understand? You know what? If you're dumber than the last guy, I'm going to have to fire you myself. This is getting ridiculous!"

"No. I'll just go get a polo." Perk heads to the kitchen and searches through the area to find a shirt. The kitchen is cluttered and not exactly clean. There are pictures and calendars taped and pinned to the walls. The theme seems to be general machismo: cars, girls in bikinis, football. Perk finds some shirts and aprons sitting on top of a shelf. He puts them on.

Near a door that looks like it leads to an office is a time clock. *Why not?* he thinks to himself and sets himself up with a time card and punches in.

Perk emerges, steps up to the cash register and, after a pause asks the cook, "What do I do?"

"Boss Man should've told you all that stuff," the cook states nonchalantly. "I just cook. I don't know any of that front of house stuff." The cook shoves the spoon into his pocket. "You can call me Compa," he says straight-faced.

"OK… Compa. I --" Perk is interrupted by the arrival of a patron. Compa quickly retreats to the sanctity of the kitchen.

A tall athletic blonde man enters and strides confidently up to the counter. "Ah," he says with a smile, "you must be the new guy."

"Apparently so."

"Name's Cal. Freelance copywriter for the paper, second floor."

"Perk." Cal and Perk shake hands. Perk nervously adds, "I should warn you, the only thing I know how to do so far is clock in."

"Well, you're miles ahead of the last guy. Man, that dude was twelve eggs short of a dozen, if you know what I mean." Cal taps his temple then laughs heartily. Perk joins in the laughter even though he doesn't quite understand the joke.

"Oh, boy. I needed that... Monday, after all." Cal gets a distant look in his eyes then snaps back. "Speaking of Monday and eggs, do you guys have chorizo yet?"

Compa chimes in from the kitchen, "I told you it'll come with the order tomorrow. I told you that after we ran out. Don't you remember, dude?"

Cal calls back to him, over Perk's shoulder. "You said it would come Tuesday and that was last Monday."

"I said it would come this Tuesday!" Compa is still in the kitchen yelling his end of the conversation. "I can't order it one day and it comes the next. What do you think this is? Some type of future place?"

Cal, in turn, yells his end of the conversation as well. "Can't you just go *buy* some chorizo from the store? Come on, this is Chorizo Monday. It's the only reason I get out of bed on Mondays!" It seems as though Cal and Compa are comfortable with this type of interaction. Still, Perk feels a bit sheepish standing silently between them.

Compa doesn't respond. Perk simply shrugs. Cal leans into Perk, "Today is Chorizo Monday and you guys don't have chorizo. I don't envy the morning you're going to have. I'll see you later, buddy... if you survive." Cal peers at Perk with steely eyes then stands straight, smiles, winks, and strides out of the café as confidently as he strode in.

Perk feels his stomach sink as he hears Cal's voice in his head saying *If you survive*. Compa emerges from the kitchen wiping his hands on a towel which he throws over his shoulder. He seems unfazed. If Chorizo Monday without chorizo is something to be feared, Compa doesn't show it.

Perk asks Compa, "What's Chorizo Monday?"

"Free chorizo and egg burritos for anyone who says, 'Today is Chorizo Monday.' It's like a promotion or something for people who work in this building. We give away like fifty of 'em every Monday. A lot of times it's to peoples who don't even work here but know about Chorizo Monday somehow. We always run out and the peoples get pissed."

"What should I tell people when they ask for one today?"

"I don't know. Like I said, I just cook stuff." Compa pauses and then continues. "Tell them they can substitute corned beef hash. We got like a ton of that. I can make it spicy if they want. Good luck, dude. I'll be in the back."

Compa turns to head back into the kitchen but stops, swings back around, looks at Perk inquisitively and asks, "You're not Carl, are you?"

"Um... no. I'm Perk."

"Oh. So you just came in and started working without even knowing what you were supposed to do?"

"I guess so."

Compa stands up straight and folds his muscular arms. He wears a V-neck T-shirt with the sleeves carelessly chopped off. "You know what?" he says with a smile revealing a gold-capped tooth at the front of his mouth, "Either you're smarter than I thought you were or dumber than I thought you were."

"I was just thinking the same thing," Perk responds with a nervous grin. "I guess we'll find out."

- • -

The following half hour yielded only a few customers wanting coffee and pastries. Perk was able to familiarize himself with the cash register and some of the menu. Things like muffins and bagels were simple, as they had the price on a small paper held by a clip on a small wire display. In addition, there was a cheat sheet of sorts -- a paper taped to the counter with the PLU's of all the items. Perk simply typed in the PLU and the item came up. Tax was programmed into the machine which made that part easy. Perk had worked at a fast food restaurant in the past so he was familiar with how cash registers worked. He also knew about making coffee, bussing, dishes, and all that standard restaurant fare. This cafe was a mom-and-pop shop, not as standardized as Perk would like, but it would do.

Perk wondered to himself how bad the previous guy had to have been to screw up a job like this. Everything seemed pretty easy and straightforward. Of course, only a half hour had passed and no food orders had been placed. As that thought went through Perk's mind, he noticed the smell of food being cooked. Between the front of the house and the kitchen was a wide cut out; a window between the two areas. Perk looked into the kitchen. Compa was cooking and dancing to Spanish music being emitted from an 80's style boom box on a shelf that housed food products.

"What are you making?" Perk asked Compa in his best I'm-not-being-nosy voice.

"Fat burrito! My specialty!" Compa continued to dance not picking up on why Perk would ask. Then he blurted out, "You hungry, dude?"

"We can eat the food here?"

"Of course, man. It ain't poisoned or anything!"

"No, I mean do we have to pay for it?"

Compa looked up at Perk and put his hands on his hips. One hand held a spatula that looked like it had been burned several times over. "Kinda... I mean, we get one free meal a day but Boss Man doesn't say how big that meal is. The way I see it, my one meal is a big meal in three courses, eaten at three different times of the day. That way I don't have to pay."

Perk wrestled with the ethics of such logic. In a strange way, it made sense. Furthermore, there was no manager to really crack down on the practice. And, by the way Compa held himself, there was probably no manager at all. But who was this *Boss Man* guy?

"Hey, Compa," Perk called out, "Who's the 'Boss Man'?"

Compa decided this was a subject that necessitated his presence in the front of the restaurant. He came through the swinging door with burrito in hand. It truly was a fat burrito, the fattest Perk had ever seen. "Boss Man is the boss, man." Compa took a bite of his burrito and continued talking with his mouth full. "Mr. Argyle. He owns this place. The whole place, building and all. I thought he would be here, seeing as how this is your first day... or the first day for the other guy but he didn't show up."

"Does Mr. Argyle come around much?"

"Not really. Maybe once a day, or once every two days." Compa took huge bites of his burrito. Perk was astonished at how quickly Compa consumed the entire thing. It was made with two large tortillas and must have had six eggs in it with potatoes.

"Who's the manager?" Perk asked.

"I guess we are." Compa burped.

Perk and Compa stood looking out at the street. People were starting to hustle back and forth, cars negotiating each other, some honking.

"I'll make you a burrito, dude." Compa said to Perk. "I'll do one of the corned beef ones all spicy so you know what you're selling."

"OK. Thanks."

Just then the door opened and a hipster ambled in.

"Today is Chorizo Monday! Hook me up!" The hipster slapped the counter with an open hand. "And give me one of those Hyper drinks. I gotta wake up!"

"Sir, we don't have chorizo. Would you like corned beef instead?"

"Corn and beef? Like a casserole or something?" The hipster eyed Perk angrily but not maliciously. "You're the new guy?"

"Yeah. Perk."

"Eugene. But you can call me 'Awesome'! Ha ha!" Eugene chuckled but still looked angry. "I guess give me one of those burritos with the corn and beef casserole. Sounds crazy but right now I'll eat anything. Up way too late last night. My band had a gig. That's right, I rock for real." Eugene paused, waiting to see if Perk was impressed. He wasn't. "I'll take the Hyper drink now though. Here." Eugene handed Perk two one dollar bills. "Keep the change." The change was nine cents. Perk placed it in a small wicker basket marked *Tips*. At this rate, with tips like that, he could finally buy a car in 35 years.

Eugene picked up a number card from the counter. It was an eight. Perk put two and two together. This was how they figured out who got what order. Perk submitted the order and wrote an eight on the ticket. He placed it in the ticket holder and swiveled it toward Compa. A bell sat next to the ticket holder. "Order in!" he called out and hit the bell. Compa danced on over and picked up the ticket and took it to the back. Apparently, this was how it was done. Easy enough.

The door opened again and an attractive woman walked gracefully to the counter. She was neatly done up and Perk could sense a hint of her perfume. He got a lump in his throat. She was wearing big sunglasses and large hoop earrings. Her thick black hair was perfectly styled as was the rest of her. "Today is Chorizo Monday." She said with as slight grin. "But they always let me get something else on account of me not eating chorizo." With that she took off her sunglasses and gave Perk a slightly flirtatious smile. "You're new," she continued, "so let me tell you what I like and how I like it." Perk gulped and felt himself blushing. This seemed to amuse the woman. "I will have a two egg white omelet with veggies, one piece of toast, and some fruit. To go. Also, a decaf peppermint hot tea, but I'll take that now. In my mug. It's the purple one." She pointed to a purple mug sitting on a wire rack amid a host of plain white mugs. She seemed accustomed to getting what she wanted and Perk was more than happy to oblige, continuing whatever special treatment she had received prior to his arrival.

"My name is Perk." Perk's voice cracked. Embarrassed he immediately broke eye contact and looked at the cash register, trying to look natural as he rung up her order.

"I am Moxy," the woman returned. "Nice to meet you." She held out her hand. Perk took it and gave it a firm shake. "Relax, cowboy. I'm not carrying any weapons. Except pepper spray but you shouldn't worry about that... or should you?" Perk looked at her wide-eyed. She was smiling and giggling. He was not used to a woman as attractive as her cutting up with him. She knew this as well as he did. She was obviously toying with him.

"Moxy. Got it. I'll put your order in. And get your tea. Here you go." Perk handed her the number seven.

"Lucky number seven," Moxy cooed. Perk felt his knees weaken a bit. Moxy turned on a heel and headed toward a counter-like surface against the window set up for dining.

Before Perk could collect his thoughts, another person came in, a dark-skinned bookish fellow with glasses, wearing a button-up shirt, tie, and vest as well as a bowler hat. "Today is Chorizo Monday!" the dapper-yet-nerdy guy called out before the door even closed behind him.

"I'll be right with you," Perk called back as he got Moxy's tea ready.

"Order up!" Compa yelled from the window.

Perk picked up Eugene's burrito and strode out to the dining area. The dapper nerd followed in tow. "Yesterweek, upon this day, the kitchen had exhausted its supply of chorizo. Now, I don't eat the chorizo myself, as I don't eat pork, yet I was told I could substitute an alternate meat item." He waited patiently as Perk served Eugene and Moxy. "Do you by chance carry corned beef hash?"

"Yes." Perk answered hastily. More people came through the door.

"Splendid! I will take a burrito with the corned beef hash with eggs. Free of charge of course. After all, I did supply you with the obligatory 'Today is Chorizo Monday' phrase." The dapper nerd stood erect with pride, a large smile on his face. He had a mustache, a soul patch, and a goatee, three entities unattached to the other. "I'll take coffee as well..." His voice trailed off in a leading way.

Perk picked up on it. "Perk." he said.

"Ah, Perk. Yes. I'll take coffee as well, Perk. My name is Wren. I am what you common folk refer to as a 'code monkey' which is ironic since your average person is more of a monkey around code than I am." With that Wren laughed loudly. Perk was not amused. He was just trying to keep up.

"Order up!" called Compa again.

More people came in, some were angry at the fact that there was no chorizo. Others were indifferent to the corned beef option, just happy to get something for free. In his mind, Perk thanked Compa for giving him that option. Today would have been hell if he had to tell people they couldn't get their free burrito.

The line at the counter was getting long. There were four people waiting impatiently as Perk did his best to take orders and deliver them to the tables. In the midst of the rush, the front doors swung open and an older, white haired lady with daggers for eyes came in walking like John Wayne. "Today is another stupid Chorizo Monday!" she exclaimed as she cut in front of a man at the head of the line. He looked angry but the woman didn't seem to care. "I'm not paying anything so I don't need to stand in line. Just give me my free burrito and I'm outta here!"

"Ma'am, if you would please take your place in line, I will be happy to -"

"I'm not paying for anything, just picking up a burrito! You should have a stack of them already made. I mean, that's what I would do if I were giving out burritos! Every Monday for three years it's been the same thing, no big stack of burritos! You always make me wait!" The woman seemed genuinely irritated. Yet the fact that she had been familiar with the process for three years didn't make sense to Perk.

"Ma'am, like I said, if you would take your place in line -"

"Tell you what, you know what I want. I'll just take a number and go over by the window. Bring me my burrito when you have it made. Understand?"

"We don't have chorizo, ma'am. If you wait in line like the rest of the -"

"No chorizo?! This happened last week too! This is an outrage! I want my money back!"

"Ma'am, you didn't pay any money."

"Well, I want something back. Give me a donut for free!"

"Ma'am, if you would let me explain, we have -"

"Get me what you can and don't call me *Ma'am*. That's my mom's name! My name is Sheryl with an 'S'. Cheryl with a 'C' in the mail room is a moron and I don't want you to get me confused with her." The woman moseyed to the window counter and angrily picked up a newspaper. Perk decided to just give her a corned beef hash and egg burrito. From what he could sense, she probably couldn't tell the difference anyway. Don't pick a battle that doesn't need to be fought.

Compa came out from the back with something in his hand. "Here, put this on so you don't have to waste all the peoples' time telling them who you are and what not." He handed Perk a name tag. The tag was black and had a name already engraved on it but it looked like Compa colored over it with a black marker. In large letters written with White-Out was scrawled "PERK". Perk shrugged and pinned it to his polo shirt. *He may be rough around the edges,* Perk thought to himself, *but that Compa guy is alright.*

- • -

The rush died down around eight-thirty. People were still eating but few new customers came in. Perk took a moment to pour himself a cup of coffee. As he was adding artificial cream and substitute sweetener he heard a young woman's voice say to him, "That stuff will kill you!" He turned around to see a pretty young woman trying to give him a mad face. Her features were soft and kind so she looked more like a baby acting tough. He couldn't help but smile.

"It's not funny," the girl said. "It *will* kill you, all those chemicals!" The girl had an earthy feel to her. She was blonde and wore a scarf to hold her hair back from her face. She was diminutive yet the slender muscles in her arms were defined. Her midriff was exposed and Perk could tell she had sparse fat on her body. "I'm not being preachy, I'm only trying to help. I'm Henna." Perk turned to her so that she could read his name tag. "Your name tag looks like a turd," she added, nose scrunched in disgust. Then she smiled and said, "I bet I could make you a name tag at work, something better than that horrid thing. I'm good at arts and crafts and I usually have a lot of free time at work." She smiled genuinely at Perk. She had crooked teeth which made her smile crooked as well. It was endearing. He tried to figure out what type of girl would volunteer to make a name tag for someone she barely met. "I mean, if you want me to that is." She fluttered her eyes in a silly attempt to be coy. Then, she grew wide-eyed and blurted out, "Today is Chorizo Monday! I'm a vegetarian! I don't eat chorizo!"

Perk tried to figure out if the girl in front of him was completely sane or not. She seemed to bounce from emotion to emotion, subject to subject. And why was she announcing she didn't eat chorizo. What was the point?

"Can I have a peanut butter and banana burrito instead and get it for free?" She tried again to look coy.

"I guess so." By this point Perk was pretty worn out. Though he had only been there for a little over two hours, he had processed several dozen people. It got busier than he thought a little cafe like that would get.

Other than Moxy's request, he had not made any other exceptions so a peanut butter and banana burrito seemed within reason. Compa complied but only with an opinion on Henna's tastes. "That chica is all hippied out, yo! She asks for the weirdest things. One time I had to make tacos made from pancakes with strawberries inside. Not just pancakes with strawberries, she insisted they were folded like tacos. She's weird."

Henna squealed with delight upon receiving her burrito. She gave Perk a five dollar tip and bounded out the door. Nice girl, he thought to himself. Not a bad shift.

- • -

The lunch rush was not as busy as breakfast. Perk handled everything in stride. One good thing about the cafe was that the menu was not complicated and Compa was pretty good about special orders. Downside was that the breakfast crowd and lunch crowd overlapped. Perk didn't get an opportunity to eat his burrito. He felt his stomach grumble. To avoid having people hear it, he asked Compa if there was any music that could be played. Compa said that was something Mr. Argyle was thinking about doing but has never done. Perk resolved to talk to his new boss about it. Perk liked music and if he was going to be acting co-manager with Compa, he would choose Paul Simon for the dining room. Compa could keep his Spanish dance tunes.

Around two-thirty, an older man came into the cafe. He walked with purpose straight up to Perk. "Carl," He said sternly, "glad to have you on board. Why does your name tag say 'Perk'? Is that a nickname or something?"

"It's kind of a nickname, sir." Perk assumed this must be Mr. Argyle. Who else could it be?

"OK, Perk it is. I hope you're getting along OK." Mr. Argyle squinted at Perk. "Wait a second…"

"I'm not Carl."

"You're not Carl. Oh, you said that. Who are you?"

"I'm Perk. I saw your ad in the paper and I came in early this morning to pick up an application. One thing led to another and I just started
working." Perk felt his confidence rise. He had maneuvered his first day
on the job without any major catastrophe.

Mr. Argyle's face softened then his brows furrowed. "Hey, Compa!"

"Sì, Boss Man?"

"Did Carl come in at all?"

"Nope. I thought Perk was Carl too."

"He does look like him. Strange." Mr. Argle peered at Perk. "So
Carl *didn't* come in but *you* came in and just started working?"

"Yes sir." Perk felt a bit nervous. Mr. Argyle's eyebrows were still
furrowed.

After what seemed to be a minute of silence, Mr. Argyle softened
his features again and held out his hand. "Name's Edwington Argyle."
Perk shook his hand. "I guess we need to get you set up properly -- W-2,
I-9, all that."

"Yes sir."

As they walked to the office in the back, Mr. Argyle turned to Perk
and said, "Not sure what to make of you just yet. What kind of person
just comes in and starts to work? It got you the job, I'll give you that
much. Still, either you're smarter than you seem, or dumber."

Perk gave a half smile and replied for the second time in one day,
"I guess we'll find out."

THE END

Party
of
Two

Is it appropriate to buy a girl underwear as a birthday present?, Perk thought to himself as he browsed the ladies section of a department store. Secretly, he wanted an excuse to make the trip down to the other end of the mall to peruse *Victoria's Secret*. As a guilty pleasure, Perk enjoyed the women's undergarment section -- be it *Victoria's Secret* or any other store -- simply as an excuse to look at the models on the labels.

Obviously such a gesture would be inappropriate. He winced at himself for even thinking it and blushed as he played the imaginary scenario in his mind. He envisioned himself presenting Nell with her birthday gift of lacy undies and having her receive them with flirtatious eyes. Of course it would not play out like that, but it was a pleasant fantasy and he held on to it for a spell.

Nell was Henna's friend. She was having a birthday party and told Henna to invite Perk. The invitation exhilarated Perk to no end. Perk had a monster crush on Nell since the first moment he laid eyes on her at the café as she and Henna were planning a work schedule for the organic farm they both volunteered at. Perk was instantly drawn to Nell. He found her small frame and big almond eyes appealing. He expected her to be more of a hippie than she was. Turns out, she volunteered at the organic farm for reasons more closely related to her religious beliefs than saving the planet. This appealed to Perk since religion was close to his heart (though he didn't wear it on his sleeve).

Although Perk received no written invitation, Henna specifically stated that the party was costume-themed. Attendees were instructed to dress as their favorite character from classic literature. Perk knew absolutely nothing about classic literature, but was doing his best to give himself a crash course. He didn't want Nell to think he was as ignorant as he really was.

Perk decided to play it safe and dress as Huckleberry Finn. He had read it as a kid and needed only a refresher to get the gist of the character. He was excited to see Nell's costume. He had seen (not read) the movie, *Pride and Prejudice* and secretly hoped Nell dressed in that fashion. He found that style sexy.

Having eliminated underwear as a gift, Perk settled on a coffee mug with an inspirational quote imprinted upon it.

"Two roads diverged in a wood, and I –
I took the one less traveled by,
And that has made all the difference." – Robert Frost

He felt the quote universal enough to be acceptable in mixed company while being vaguely specific to her faith… at least that's how he read it in his mind.

The party started at 7:30 PM, Saturday. It was 2:00 PM that same Saturday when Perk finally purchased the gift. He had a habit of procrastination. The outfit was next. All he needed for that was some old oversized pants cuffed up to the calf held up with suspenders, an oversized button-up shirt, a corncob pipe and a hat with frayed edges. He had the hat already – purchased at a second-hand store earlier that day. He felt proud about knocking that out early even though it was still in the eleventh hour.

The rest of the afternoon involved Perk getting his costume ready, buying a six pack of beer and making the closest thing to a "potluck dish" that he could muster – chips and dip. He was anxious and happy, nervous and excited.

Meanwhile, Nell was in the midst of an unfortunate situation. Earlier that morning, her cat Nickel had escaped the safety of the house and ran into the street and into the path of an oncoming car. Needless to say, Nickel gave up the ghost.

Because of Nickel's demise, Nell canceled the party. This information, however, did not reach Perk. Henna had invited Perk in person at the café and didn't know how to get in touch with him as she did not have his phone number. Henna either thought Perk would magically find out or he wouldn't show up. Or maybe she simply didn't care. Most likely the latter since her carefree disposition disregarded such details.

Perk had not found out. As far as he knew, the party was still on. Even worse, he grew increasingly excited. He was so excited that he decided to head over to Nell's early. *Maybe she'll need help setting up,* he thought to himself, not realizing the risk of a social faux pas. *She might think of me as a gentleman.* He dwelt on that fantasy for a few minutes with a goofy grin slapped on his face.

Perk walked the two miles to Nell's house so that he wouldn't have to ride the bus in his outfit. Somehow, walking in the Huck clothes seemed more acceptable. He arrived at her house at 6:45 PM. It did not surprise him in the least that there were no other cars congregated on the street. Why would it? The party didn't start for another 45 minutes.

He ambled to the door using his best *cool guy* walk. What if she happened to be looking out the window? He rang the doorbell. No answer. So, he knocked. No answer. *Odd,* he thought. He rang the doorbell again. A few seconds later, Nell answered.

"Hi!" Perk said loudly. "Thought I'd come by early, see if you needed help."

Nell stood there stunned and peered at Perk. It took her a few seconds to process what had happened – no one told him the party had been canceled. So, here stood a guy dressed like a redneck hobo beaming from ear to ear. And while the unfortunate demise of Nickel still lingered, Nell couldn't help but chuckle at Perk. He seemed so harmless and happy.

"Please come in," Nell said, still chuckling. Perk noticed she was not yet in costume. *She must need my help,* he thought to himself and added some brownie points to his own tally.

Inside, the house was anything but party-ready. A blanket and a pillow lay disheveled in a heap on the couch. Someone was laying around watching TV. *The nerve of her roommate!,* Perk thought to himself. *Watching TV when she should be helping Nell decorate!*

"Have a seat," Nell said, gesturing to the couch. "Don't mind my mess." Perk was confused. Nell went into the kitchen and came back with two glasses of water and sat next to him.

"I guess Henna didn't tell you," she said.

"Tell me what?"

"The party… my cat… canceled."

"Your cat canceled the party?" Perk asked innocently and inquisitively.

"Not exactly. The party is canceled *because* of my cat. Nickel, that's his – that *was* his name. He died today."

"Oh."

"Yeah. He got out this morning and a car hit him. Hit and run, though you never know if the person even felt it. Could have been a truck or something, you know?" Nell was looking down, but not crying. Perk noticed that her voice was even and calm. He thought it strange that she wasn't shedding tears. After all, her cat was dead. Then again, she could have been crying all day or perhaps be in shock.

"He was skinny," Nell said straightforwardly. "I bet even a small car wouldn't have felt the bump. Maybe it wasn't a bump. Maybe he just got hit or something." Nell continued with a logical approach. It seemed a bit cold. Perk just sat and listened.

"I canceled the party after we found him on the side of the road. I told Henna. Kinda figured she'd tell you."

"I don't have her number. Don't think she has mine."

"Ah." They sat in silence for a moment.

"Well, *I* feel like an idiot," Perk said honestly.

"You didn't know. You couldn't have."

"I feel like an idiot dressed like this for no reason. No reason now, that is."

"I like your costume, Huck." Nell smiled at Perk. He blushed. "Thank you for dressing up. You're a good sport. I half expected people to not dress up or half-ass it." Perk had felt he half-assed it himself, although he would never admit it to Nell.

"What was going to be your costume?" He asked.

"Captain Nemo."

"But wasn't Captain Nemo a guy?"

"I know that, silly. I was going to be a sexy *female* version of Captain Nemo."

"Isn't that cheating? Why not be someone from *Pride and Prejudice* or something?"

"Like a sexy female version of Elton?"

"No, like—" Perk noticed her wry smile and realized she was messing with him. Her big soft almond eyes glinted. He was mesmerized by them.

"Wanna see my outfit?" Nell blurted with a spark.

"Sure, I guess. I mean, are you OK? Your cat and all?"

"Yeah, I'm OK. I have to show it to someone, right? It would be a shame *not* to." Nell jumped up and ran out of the room excitedly. She seemed spry. Perk sat uncomfortably. He felt silly in his Huck Finn adornment. It seemed to take Nell longer than he thought it should take. All she had to do was pick up the outfit and bring it into the living room, right? *Maybe she needed to use the bathroom,* he thought to himself. *She wasn't expecting me. Maybe I caught her at a bad time. I don't like people visiting me when I need to use the bathroom.*

Nell called out, "Are you ready?"

"Yeah." Ready for what?

Nell strode into the living room with all the confidence of a sea captain. She was wearing the costume and had applied a touch of make-up for effect. "Ahoy!" she said loudly and gave a half smile. Perk smiled at the sight of her. She was, in fact, a sexy female version of Captain Nemo, or at least she was a sexy version of something. Perk wasn't all that familiar with Captain Nemo so he simply smiled at the presence of a pretty girl having fun in a costume. She *did* look good though.

"The state of these quarters is unacceptable!" she said in a loud voice and looked down her nose at the blankets on the couch. "This vessel is the finest on any sea, be it on the surface or below. I shall not allow lackadaisical behavior. It is a contagion that must be eliminated!" She glared at Perk sternly then broke character and laughed. "You look so scared," she said to him.

"I thought you were going to feed me to the sharks," Perk replied. She laughed even more heartily at this comment. Then she spread out her arms and spun around. "Well?" she asked, fishing for a compliment.

"You look great! I mean your outfit. I mean you in your outfit– and your outfit. Both look great. You know what I mean."

"I do, Huck." She picked up the blanket and pillow, tossed them onto a chair and plopped down beside him. "What did you bring for the party?"

"I guess it doesn't matter, but I brought some chips and dip and a six pack of New Belgium 1554. Thought the beer would fit the theme. Probably not the chips and dip. Don't know when those were invented."

"Break out the goods!" Nell said.

Perk didn't argue. He took out each item methodically and placed them on the coffee table.

Nell sat up straight. "Ale, Huck?" she said in character. "Why, I'm sure a boy your age would not imbibe such spirits."

"Ain't a boy," Perk retorted in his best Huck Finn Missouri southerner voice. "Least not in here," he tapped his temple with his finger. "Nor in here either," he thumped his heart with his fist and sat straight and proud. "If'n y'knew all the 'ventures I done gone through, why, you'd assume I was as old as the world itself." Nell sat wide eyed and gaped happily as Perk played along with her.

"Very well," Nell announced. "I see no reason to keep such a seasoned venerable veteran of worldly exploits such as yourself from enjoying a swig of ale." She broke character again and squeezed his arm. "I'll be right back," she said as she jumped up and ran into the kitchen. Perk liked how she ran inside, almost like a child at play. She came back with a bottle opener and some napkins.

"I was thinking," Perk said, "since we're both dressed up and it's still your birthday, why not have a mini party?" Perk felt surprised that the words came out of his mouth. It wasn't boldness but rather a lack of a filter.

Nell stood and stared up to the left then to the right as if looking at the stars in the sky. "OK," she said. "But you have to help me decorate."

Perk agreed. Decorating did not take long at all. The room had Christmas lights up around the perimeter of the ceiling. She added some streamers and some confetti and placed classic literature books here and there. Then she brought out some action figures and put them on the table.

"What are those?" Perk asked.

"My nerd toys," she answered and held them up one by one. "This one is Charles Dickens. This one is Shakespeare. This is Oscar Wilde. And this one, by far my favorite, is Jane Austen." She stood them up on the table.

Nell turned off all the lights in the living room and plugged in the Christmas lights. The room was engulfed in a soft yellow glow.

"Oooh," they both cooed at the same time, which made them laugh.

"Time for tunes!" Nell jumped up and put a record on a vintage phonograph player. It was classical music.

"Who's this?" Perk asked.

"Beethoven."

"That's him playing?"

"No! That's impossible. He's the composer. Someone else is playing."

"I obviously don't know a lot about classical music," Perk lamented feeling a bit deflated and dumb.

"You don't need to. It's more about feeling than understanding." Nell sat down next to Perk, closer than before. She seemed to like being near him. "I mean, there's the theory of the music: notes, chords, progression, time signatures, all that. But sometimes that heady stuff can take away from the emotion that the composers are conveying. It's like trying to copy and edit a love letter for grammar."

Perk could see how passionate Nell was about classic books, music, clothing, and such. Her passion was intoxicating.

"First party game," Nell announced. "Tell us a little about yourself."

"OK," Perk was willing to play along. "My name is Perk. I work at a café—"

"No! Not about you, about your character. About Huck!"

"Oh!" Perk stood up and put his thumbs in his suspenders. "See? I was born an old soul, set on wanderin'. At the same time, I ain't ever gonna grow up. No sir, not me. Not Huck." He had some theater experience in high school and he put it to good use, exaggerating his actions and projecting his voice. Nell giggled and leaned forward with her elbows on her knees, holding her beer loosely and casually. He continued, "Why, all's a man's got in this world is his freedom. Take that away, take away the man from the man. All's left is a shell. Plenty folk just shells walking up and down the street. Not me. No sir, not Huck. I'm as free as a bird. Freer in fact cuz I got me this," he tapped his temple again. "And you, Cap'n?"

Nell stood up as Perk took a seat. She began in dramatic fashion. "As I mentioned before, this is my vessel. By that, I mean to say I am captain and proprietor. Like you, I esteem freedom highly. I go where I desire, do what I wish and get paid handsomely to allow others to share in my escapades. And while I have only been seagoing for the past 25 years, I was born a captain. The world simply needed to come to terms with that fact." Nell gave her speech while pacing back and forth in front of Perk, like a colonel in front of a regiment. Similar to Nell, Perk was now leaning forward in his seat, fawning.

The two of them played a memory game with cards bearing the likeness of classical authors. Nell was giddy. If she was upset about Nickel, she didn't show it.

"Want to listen to something different? I know some people don't like classical all that much."

"I'm OK with it. I'm having fun."

"I am too," Nell said, then paused. "I guess I shouldn't be having fun, but I am. Can I tell you something? Something horrible?"

"OK."

"But promise you won't think I'm a monster."

"OK."

"My cat, Nickel... I'm not really as broken up as I should be," she pursed her lips. "I inherited him from my old roommate. He wasn't mine to begin with. And..." she looked away from Perk. "I... I kinda didn't like him at all. I didn't want him to die though." Perk sat and listened. "Part of me is happy that he's gone. It sounds completely horrible, I know. I feel like a jerk. Admitting it makes everything seem even worse."

"Then, why..."

"Why cancel the party?"

"Yeah."

"Because everyone expected it. I called my mom to tell her about Nickel and she said, 'What a shame. Well, it wouldn't be right to have fun on such a sad day.' Then, some of my friends said basically the same thing. And through it all, I was thinking to myself, We should celebrate *because* Nickel's gone. I know that sounds completely monstrous for me to say, but it's kinda true. He was a total terror! He would scratch at everything... my drapes, my furniture." She pointed to the arm of the couch. It was ripped up but the frayed edges had been trimmed neatly. "He would jump on my face to wake me up. One time he scratched me, right here." She pointed to her eyebrow. "He could have scratched my eyeball and blinded me or something!" Nell's brows furrowed. A moment passed and her features softened. "I used to tell him all the time that I wished he would get hit by a car. Then it actually happened. It's a weird feeling, you know? Wishing for something bad to happen and then it does. You don't know whether to feel satisfied or guilty. I guess I feel both." She stopped for a moment then blurted out, "I must sound like a psychopath!"

"No, not at all," Perk said. "You sound honest."

"You're sweet." They sat for a moment, not speaking. Nell broke the silence. "Sooo… let's play another game!"

"OK."

Nell led Perk through a series of games. Some were meant for a group so she changed the rules around ever so slightly to accommodate two people. With the weight of Nickel off of her shoulders, Nell was carefree and fun. Perk made jokes and Nell giggled at each one. Perk took this as a good sign, that Nell might be up for something more than just a one-time deal.

The six pack was now reduced to one beer that sat on the table among chips and dip and action figures and games and confetti. Nell picked up the beer, opened it and took a swig. She placed another record on the record player. It was a choral piece, a cappella. She sat down next to Perk on the couch, touching shoulder to shoulder. "I had to have this record pressed myself," she said. "There's a place online that presses vinyl. These guys are newer, so they don't really have any vinyl available. I love vinyl." She got a faraway look in her eyes as if she was experiencing a joyful memory from childhood. Perk's heart leapt inside his chest as he felt her warm arm touching his. He liked listening to her as much as he liked looking at her.

He pursed his lips and said, "I think…" This broke Nell's trance.

"You think what?" Nell asked as she turned to him.

"I… " Perk's heart raced and his voice broke a little. It was now or never. He placed his hand on hers and leaned in to kiss her. She pulled away.

"Oh, I… we can't," she stammered. "I'm seeing someone. It wouldn't be right." She pulled her hand out from under his and slid further down the couch. He instinctively sat on his hands.

"Seeing someone? It didn't… doesn't seem like it. You didn't say anything. I mean, he's not here." He looked at her inquisitively.

"Yeah. It's kinda new. I told him I wanted to be alone. I did want to be alone after calling off the party. I thought it would be best. I've been watching Netflix all day. Then, you came and I realized I *did* want company."

"We were having so much fun."

"Yes, we were. We are. I'm sorry. I like you, I do. And I am having a blast," she paused. "And truth be told, I would like to kiss you," she blushed. "But it's not right. It just wouldn't be right."

"I understand," Perk said softly. "I feel like a turd." Nell was in the middle of taking a drink of beer as he told her this. His use of the word "turd" at such a sensitive moment made her laugh, which in turn, made her spit her beer. She covered her mouth as she continued to laugh.

"It almost came out of my nose!" she said and punched Perk in the shoulder. He didn't know what was so funny, but began to laugh at the sight and sound of her giggling and cleaning up.

After she collected herself, she turned her body to Perk and pulled his hands out from under his thighs and held them in her hands. "I like you, Perk. I liked you back when I met you when I was with Henna. I wasn't attached at that point. If all this happened back then…" she smiled at him. Her eyes glowed and shimmered in the soft light. He couldn't be sure, but he thought her eyes were welling up. "It's just bad timing." She held his face in her hand and kissed him on the cheek.

Perk smiled and shrugged. He donned the Huck character and said, "Reckon a kiss on the cheek from a princess is more than a po' boy like ol' Huck deserves."

Nell smiled and shook her head. "Oh, Huck, you deserve so much more." She gave him a long hug.

"You didn't open your gift," Perk said and handed her the bag. Nell opened it up and read the message on the mug.

"I love it," she said. "Road less traveled, taking chances." She frowned then smiled and squeezed Perk's hand. "Thank you," her voice cracked.

"You're welcome."

- • -

The two mile walk home was bittersweet for Perk. On one hand, he struck out with possibly the neatest chick he had ever met. On the other hand, she genuinely did seem to like him.

"Timing," he said out loud and kicked a pine cone on the sidewalk. Somewhere in the distance, a dog barked and a siren whined. Life continued as before.

Perk was still single, yet his hope had advanced ever so slightly. Maybe he could have a chance with a girl like Nell. Maybe even Nell herself if the stars aligned themselves just right. He thought of how much she liked the classics: classical music, classical literature, vinyl records. And he thought of how she handled the situation. Everything about her was classy, like Audrey Hepburn or Jackie O.

"Well, Huck," he told himself, "Life is just one adventure after another. If there's nothing at this point of the river, I reckon there's gotta be something up around the bend." He stopped and looked at the stars. "Trick is to keep paddlin'." He smiled to himself, put his hands in his pockets and headed home.

THE END

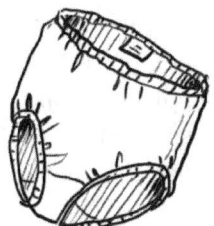

"You're smokin', Foxy! How about you and me make some heat together?" The comment came from over Moxy's right shoulder. It was a man's voice, saturated with bravado. The music in the club was loud. This comment was spoken directly to her, in her ear. She could feel the heat from his breath and smell the, what was that? Jägermeister?

What sort of come on is that? Moxy thought to herself. "I'm good," she said nonchalantly without turning to see her pursuer.

"I *know* you're good," he responded. "I'm thinking I could make you *better.*"

Moxy turned on her barstool to engage the guy. He was good-looking; twenty-something with a chiseled chin and a cocky expression. He smiled smugly, looking down his nose at her. "I'm perfectly fine without your... input, thank you. Now scoot!" Moxy waved him off. As he walked away, she heard him laugh and repeat, "Input!" It occurred to Moxy that he gave up rather easily until she saw him approach another girl without missing a beat. *Player,* she thought to herself.

Chelsea, Moxy's club buddy for the night looked disgusted. "Why did you have to be so rude to that guy? He was hot!"

"Oh, come on!" Moxy returned, "He was cocky as all get out. 'Foxy'? Really?"

"I like 'em cocky."

"You can have him. Want me to go over there, get him, and bring him back for you?"

"Would you?"

"Chelsea!"

"What?! Oh... you were kidding? Sometimes I don't know with you." Chelsea sipped her blue vodka martini. Moxy nursed her own drink: a blended margarita in a brandy snifter.

"Don't you get just a teensy bit sick of guys hitting on you just for your looks?" Moxy asked Chelsea earnestly.

""He didn't hit on *me*. Like every other guy, he hit on *you* first!" Chelsea over exaggerated a pout. "And," she continued, "he didn't even hit on me when you rejected him. I didn't even get your table scraps."

"You get hit on plenty. Don't be a baby."

"I get hit on when I'm not with you or when some guy is talking you up and I'm sitting here sipping my drink on the side like some sort of third wheel loser."

This gave Moxy pause. She wasn't aware of the fact that guys hit on her first, and that Chelsea -- or maybe any other of her girlfriends -- got irritated because of it.

Moxy knew she was attractive and she leveraged it whenever and wherever possible. She worked hard at being pretty and it had served her well. Guys bought her drinks, took her out to nice places, gifts, shows, the works. And not just from suitors or wannabe suitors. Her clients practically begged to have her sell to them -- her male clients a least. Moxy's success as an advertising sales representative for a local publisher hinged on her attractiveness and, to a lesser extent, her charisma. She had the top sales of any salesperson in the field. And she was well aware that they weren't buying because her pitch was perfect. After all, her lead was simply, "Hiya, sweetie!"

Is it wrong to leverage my looks for attention and... money? She thought to herself. Outwardly she frowned and stared off into the distance as the gears in her head turned.

"Earth to Moxy. Hello," Chelsea sounded irritated.

"Oh, sorry," Moxy said as she realized she was deep in thought and ignoring Chelsea.

"Moxy, sometimes I just don't get you!" Chelsea looked around the room. "I mean, guys aren't as attracted to me as they are to you—I'm OK with that, I get my fair share. But sometimes it seems like you actually don't like guys hitting on you."

"Not guys like that. He only talked to me because he thought I looked good."

"Duh!" Chelsea put down her drink. She had a way of expressing herself with her hands and had wasted too many drinks due to spillage during a rant. True to form, she started waving her hands in front of her as she talked. "We're not here for the rocket scientist convention! It's a club for Pete's sake!"

"I know that! But don't you ever get tired of getting hit on just for your looks?"

"No! And it's because I'm not stupid!"

"Hearing you talk like that kind of gives me the creeps." Moxy scrunched her face. "It's like you buy into the shallowness of it all."

"Buy into it? It's called life, honey." Chelsea put her hands in her lap and turned toward Moxy as if talking to a child. "Do guys hit on us because we're hot? Of course. Do I want a guy to like me for more than my tatas?" She leaned back and cupped her breasts in her hands. She tended to forget she was in public when she got deep into conversation. "Yes, I would. But the best way to get to my heart is through the tatas." She jiggled her breasts up and down. Moxy blushed and felt her face grow warm with embarrassment. She looked around to see if anyone was witnessing Chelsea's uncouth behavior. In private Moxy might behave as such but never in public. It was, in her opinion, unladylike. As Moxy's eyes scanned the room, she noticed a few sets of eyes peering in their direction. One guy, a fat dark man cupped his own hefty breasts and winked. Moxy groaned but Chelsea didn't even register it.

"Think about it," Chelsea continued. She turned her attention back to her blue martini, took another sip. The drink was still cold and strong on her tongue. "Mmm," she said, distracted. She paused a beat then regained her thoughts. "Think about it. How is the guy going to ever get to know you if he doesn't approach you? And the best way to get him to approach you is to lure him with beauty. Guys won't come talk to us because they can magically know we're smart or something." She curled her hair with her finger. "Never works like that for me."

"That's because neither of us are particularly smart."

"Speak for yourself, dummy! I've got mad smarts! I've memorized five movies!"

"Well, excuuuuse me, Einstein!"

"That's what I thought." Chelsea sipped her drink and looked around the club hopefully. Moxy knew that look. Chelsea wanted to get hit on, just once so the night wouldn't be a complete waste.

- • -

The next day, Moxy was haunted by her thoughts. Was she as shallow as the guys at the clubs?

While getting herself dolled up for the day, she paused every so often to observe herself in the mirror. Such care and attention had been given to her appearance, yet, until now, she had not noticed how *much* care and attention.

A memory overtook her. She was twelve and in middle school, sixth grade pre-algebra with Mrs. Grady. Mrs. Grady's student teacher was a young man named Robert. Moxy remembered how he insisted on being called by his first name. For the life of her, she couldn't remember his last name. Not that it mattered.

As with most young girls, the presence of an older, attractive guy excited her. Robert was in his early twenties, handsome and clean cut. She remembered the scent of his cologne; masculine and enticing. She had a schoolgirl crush on him. But which schoolgirl hadn't?

Robert played a few roles in Mrs. Grady's class. He assisted in grading papers, filling in teaching when she was out of the classroom and, most notably in Moxy's memory, a tutor. Robert sat at a low table at the left of the room that was his work station. When a kid needed help with a problem, they were encouraged to seek assistance with Robert. The kid would sit beside him as he helped them work through their confusion. Needless to say, Moxy somehow had more than her fair share of math problems. Many of which were not problems at all, simply excuses to sit next to Robert and sense his presence beside her.

Some days, Mrs. Grady excused herself from the room and left Robert in the role of babysitter—there was no lesson to be given. The kids were merely told to work on homework until she got back. It was assumed that these were smoke breaks as the pungent smell of Mrs. Grady's cigarette breath wafted through time and space by way of a memory. Moxy scrunched up her nose in disgust and forced her mind back on the infinitely more pleasant memory of Robert.

It was a cold gray day when Mrs. Grady went on another such excursion from the classroom. The kids never really behaved yet they weren't excessively rowdy. The girls wouldn't dare seem too uncouth in front of Robert and the boys didn't want to seem too immature, just enough on both sides. So, they talked and joked. Only a nerd or two actually used the time for homework.

Moxy, though far from being a nerd herself, used this opportunity to do her math homework… in a way that is. She feigned confusion to any random math problem conveniently at hand.

"Robert," she asked with doe eyes, "can you help me with something?"

"Sure." His voice was low and deep. She could almost feel it vibrating in her chest as he spoke.

She sat beside him, close. "I don't understand, 'What is 10% of 50.' If

'What' is 'x' and 'is' is 'equals,' then 'x' equals ten times 50? That's 500. Is that right?"

Robert grinned. He knew what was going on. "What's weird is that you actually think I'm convinced you need help."

Moxy blushed. "But... I do. I'm confused about percentages." She looked around the room to see if anyone noticed her blush. Only a few envious girls looked their way.

"You used this same equation last week to ask another question. Remember? You said, 'I know five is 10% of 50...'"

Moxy was caught. She sat silent.

"Moxy, you're not nearly as ditsy as you put on. Why are you faking it?" She didn't respond. "Look, I'm not stupid," Robert said with a smirk. "I know that you make like you're bad at math so that you can come sit near me. It's obvious," he leaned in and whispered, "you have a schoolgirl crush on me."

Moxy blushed again, "What? No way, weirdo!" She tried to look disgusted, but couldn't help but smile at him as he sat grinning in self-satisfaction. "I think," she continued with as much arrogance as she could muster, "that *you're* the one who has a crush on *me.*" She sat up straight-backed and proud in her chair with her hands neatly placed upon her lap.

"That would not be appropriate for man my age," he replied in a professional tone. Then added, "Yet, if I were not a man my age, yes, I would have a crush on you. Just like all these boys do." He made a wave gesture with his hand across the room. "And like all these boys here, you would be out of my league. You don't know it, but you've got it."

"Got what?" Moxy asked intrigued, suddenly warmed back up to him.

"Je ne sais quoi, that certain trait that can only be described as having... 'It.' You're going to be a heart breaker if you aren't one already." He put his hand on his heart and play-acted as if he were having a heart attack.

From that moment on, Moxy was conscious of her *je ne sais quoi,* as Robert put it. To hear the one guy that every girl had a crush on say that she was out of his league filled her with pride and confidence. It wasn't until now, standing there looking at her adult self in the mirror, that she gave any thought to the downside of such an existence.

She had to admit it: her body was amazing. Her muscles were toned and lean from a dedicated exercise regiment. Her dimensions were curvy and shapely. Her skin was a clear and uniform olive color -- only the best skin care products. She instinctively assumed a few different poses to observe more deeply. Yes, she was a fine specimen. Guys did, in fact, desire her and she turned down the majority of them.

But had she placed too much stock in her physical appearance? Is this all there is to her being? A pretty face and a rockin' bod? It was at that moment, mid Marilyn Monroe pose, that Moxy decided to do an experiment: *Operation: Frumpy Girl.* Execution date: Next Saturday.

The plan was simple. Dress up as frumpy and unattractive as possible to see if she could get a guy to hit on her based solely on her mind or personality.

- • -

While the plan was simple, the execution proved tougher than expected. Better put, there was an unexpected extent of both ease and difficulty. Buying frumpy clothes proved to be the easiest stage of the plan. In fact, this was actually fun for Moxy. She enlisted the help of Jessica, the closest thing to a hippie in her circle of friends.

Jessica only wore second-hand clothing. She didn't believe in buying anything new, except for food and kitchen items, for Jessica was a foodie variety of hippie. And while Jessica dressed in second-hand clothing, she was far from frumpy. She had a natural beauty, slender and blonde with finely tanned brown skin from working outdoors in community gardens. Her hair was streaked and wavy, healthy and appealing. Moxy had read *Clan of the Cave Bear* and though Jessica would make a perfect Ayla.

Moxy treated Jessica to tea as a prepayment for assistance. "Jess," Moxy started after small talk, "I need your help. I need to get old, frumpy clothes. The kind ugly girls wear."

Jessica looked insulted.

"I'm not saying *you're* ugly or *your* clothes are frumpy," Moxy corrected herself somewhat ungracefully. "I just need to know where to get gross looking second-hand clothes."

Jessica's countenance softened and then became inquisitive. "Why?"

"I…" Moxy paused. All of a sudden the idea seemed outwardly humiliating. Yet, isn't this exactly why the experiment has to happen? To embrace humility? "I'm doing an experiment. I want to get ugly. Only for a day, that is."

"And what do you hope to gain from this experiment? Empathy with the attractive-impaired?" Jessica looked self-righteously down her nose at Moxy. For all her equality talk, Jessica had a way of coming across as elitist.

"It's more about finding out something about myself. Internal." Moxy bit her lip. "I want to see if I rely too heavily on my looks."

Jess came back down to Moxy's level and smiled. "Oh, honey, you're *all* about your looks. Everyone knows that."

Moxy frowned. "I'm not *all* about looks, am I? I mean, there's more to me. Don't you think?"

"Sure, sure." Jessica paused. "Believe me, if there wasn't anything more to you than a pretty face, I wouldn't hang out with you. You know how big I am on substance."

"You mean substanc*es,* don't you, hippie?" Moxy gave a wry smile.

"Don't judge me," Jessica said playfully. "This isn't about me, it's about you." Jessica sipped her tea and looked off into the distance before continuing. "So, you want to take a… vanity fast?"

"I hadn't thought of it like that, but yeah, sure. I'll go with that."

"Solid! Let's get you grubby!" Jessica grabbed Moxy's hand and pulled her out of her seat, abandoning their still steaming beverages.

- • -

Moxy and Jess embarked on Second Handsome Luke's a hip used clothing store in the downtown area. And while the clothes were used, unfortunately all their clothes were stylish, nothing frumpy.

They moved onto Econo Closet. This was a consignment place, something like a large yard sale yet indoors. A few ugly pieces, but no true gems to speak of.

Then, they hit Save Lots. Jackpot! Moxy and Jess loaded up on dozens of old, stretched out, goofy clothes. Moxy knew this was only a one-day thing, but she also was well aware that the perfect outfit is usually found hidden within dozens of pieces.

The two of them returned to Moxy's condo. Moxy was excited and stripped down to her underwear. "OK, do me up!" she said to Jess.

"Hold up!" Jess said abruptly holding her hands in a *stop* gesture in front of her. "Two things: First, you better wash these before putting them on. Trust me. My friend Allison once got scabies from a pre-owned skirt. Second, do you have any frumpier underwear? I mean, look at you! You're like a freakin' ad for lingerie!"

Moxy looked down at her fine underwear. It was a high thread count black set with intricately woven lace adorning the edges, each piece fit snug and perfect. "Who cares what my underwear looks like? No one's going to see it."

"But *you'll* know and it will affect you. Nice underwear does that, makes you feel secretly sexy. So does no underwear," Jessica winked.

"Well, I'm not wearing used underwear, that's for sure!"

"You don't need used, just frumpy." Jess hooked her index finger on Moxy's bra from the front and snapped it violently. Moxy fumed. Jess looked sternly at Moxy and demanded, "Go get yourself a cheap bra and package of panties from the mall."

"Package?"

"Yes, Moxy, cheap underwear comes in packages."

"Oh." Moxy felt foolish. She had been particular about her underwear since middle school, only purchasing the finest pieces form the best stores. In fact, she avoided department store ladies undergarment sections like the plague. She didn't want to be perusing the *slums* as she called them. *Wow,* she thought to herself, *I really* am *vain.*

True to her go-all-out character, Moxy purchased the cheapest, ugliest bra she could find. The tag didn't even have a model. She also picked up a package of high-waisted, polyester, skin tone panties. As a pre-experiment, she wore them under her normal clothes for a day at work. Jessica was correct. Wearing the not-so-sexy underwear did have an effect on Moxy's overall confidence (or lack thereof). The cheap bra didn't hug her breasts nearly as nice as her usual fare. And it kind of hurt. The panties were down-right horrendous. Not only did they look matronly but, when she wore them under her clothes, they bunched up and somehow, at the same time, slid around by themselves. It occurred to Moxy that this bunching and shifting might be attributed to the fact that much of her clothing was tight fitting and meant to be worn with thongs and undergarments of the like. Needless to say, Moxy felt anything but sexy.

On the Saturday morning of her grand experiment, Moxy got herself donned completely in a frumpy outfit, inside and out. Of course there was the underwear, which, although new, was already losing some of it's elasticity. She wore beige polyester pants with an elastic waist. Up top, she wore a purple oversized sweatshirt with a print of a cartoon chicken on it saying, "I'm a CHEEP date!" Under that, she wore a green polo with the collar poking out up top. She tried to strap a pillow to her midsection to give the impression of fat, but it looked fake since her face, hands and legs told the truth. But even without the pillow, she accomplished a frumpy look with the faded, ill-fitting garments.

For shoes, Moxy wore her beach flip-flops. They were blue and looked out of place with the outfit. Other than the fact that her toenails were immaculate, the ensemble was convincing enough. Her forecast for the day was both positive and negative. An odd feeling. A new feeling. An experience.

Next up: face and hair. Even without make-up, her face was attractive -- a mix of fine, delicate features mixed with bold lines. To combat this, she used the age-old masking method of, you guessed it, wearing glasses. She had the foresight to think of this tactic at the second-hand store. She had picked up a pair of old, large-rimmed glasses and popped out the lenses -- ironically, she wouldn't be able to see with the lenses in. No one would get close enough to notice. As a final touch, she added some scotch tape to one end of the frames. She made it look as if it were done in a way to conceal the fact, as one who wore glasses presumably would do as well. She couldn't fashion her hair in any way that would look naturally neglected so she pulled it all back and purposely pulled some strands out to give a frazzled look. Last piece, an old black fanny pack. Yuck! The end result was not as ugly as she would have liked, but definitely frumpy. She did not feel sexy. "Mission accomplished," she said looking in the mirror.

She methodically planned her day. First she would patronize a coffeehouse in a high end neighborhood. Next, the farmer's market. Third, grocery shopping. Fourth, an al fresco lunch downtown at a patio café with plenty of foot traffic. Fifth, a museum and art gallery. Sixth, the mall with the bulk of that visit in the large book store. Last stop, a wine and beer pub, popular with the college crowd. A few of these places had yielded a surplus of guys hitting on her when she was in her normal attire and adornment.

She hopped into her car and headed out. As she approached her first destination, she breathed deeply and said to no one in particular, "Let's see what they think of me now."

The first thing she noticed about the coffeehouse was that no one noticed her. Even when she bellied up to the counter, the baristas ignored her and continued talking amongst themselves. This came as a shock since she thought people would gasp at how different she now appeared. Then it hit her—why would they be shocked? After all, no one knew what she looked like on any other day. For all they knew, she dressed like this all the time. Again, the sting of vanity pricked her.

She waited at the counter for what seemed like five minutes; though her concept of time may be skewed by her current preoccupied mindset. She was finally tended to by a female barista who greeted her with a smirk. "What'll you have?" the barista asked looking over Moxy's shoulder at the line.

"I'll take—" Moxy was interrupted by a male barista leaning over the female barista's shoulder and whispered something in her ear. This made the female barista giggle.

"What was that?" the female barista asked distracted. "I didn't get it." Moxy hadn't even ordered.

"Hot tea, decaf, for here," Moxy said slightly peeved. The girl rang up the order, all the while giving her attention elsewhere. Moxy felt invisible. Normally, she got treated well by both male and female cashiers. She felt like dog poop.

She sat at a table and sipped her tea. She had a newspaper on the table that she casually glanced at here and there. She wanted to look approachable. In her mind, she figured that uglier guys might hit on her since guys naturally hit on the girls of similar attractiveness or, in this case, unattractiveness. Again, the feeling of vanity waved over her.

She scanned the coffee shop for guys who might fit the bill in terms of level of attractiveness… or lack thereof. She was surprised at the faces she saw. Looking at people intently was, well, eye opening. A guy in the corner was writing in a journal, seemingly oblivious to the world. He wore a faded brown jacket and his hair was careless and tussled. He wasn't exactly *hot* yet there was a steely handsomeness to his features. Moxy had never seen him here before, or rather, she never noticed him. She had never really noticed any of the people. Guys noticed her and approached. Why waste energy searching for guys when they came to her? Moxy continued to scan. The coffee shop was filled with people of varying levels of age and attractiveness. There were two girls sitting and sipping their hot drinks. Moxy analyzed them. Neither would turn heads on the street yet they talked gaily and giggled. Looking at how the girls were dressed—worn jeans, hoodies, hair pulled back haphazardly—Moxy thought to herself, *I wouldn't be caught dead leaving the house looking like that!* Then, of course, reality set in and she looked down at her clothes. "Oh," she said aloud.

She spotted some potential candidates, a couple of guys talking excitedly over papers strewn across their table. "A *five* and a *six*," she said to herself and sat up straight hoping to get their attention. The two guys seemed oblivious to her.

After a few minutes, she stirred her tea loudly, the spoon clinking against the sides of the ceramic mug. One of the guys, the *six,* looked her way. She smiled. The guy grinned, then quickly turned his attention back to his partner. "Hm!" Moxy exclaimed disappointed.

Another few minutes passed. Moxy pulled out the big guns she pretended to be reading the paper and then laughed as if she read something funny. "Hahaha… oh my! I can't believe it!" she said loud enough for the *six* to hear. Again, he glanced at her, then quickly back to his table. *He's afraid to come talk to me,* she thought to herself. *That's adorably pitiful.*

Time was running out at Spot #1. Aside from the fleeting glances from the *six,* no one seemed to even acknowledge her existence. *The day is early,* she thought to herself as she gathered her things and headed out to Spot #2.

The Farmer's Market was held each Saturday at Memorial Park near the center of town. The market was packed with people: couples, families, dog walkers, hipsters, grandparents, you name it. This Saturday looked busier than normal. *I'm bound to catch a bite,* Moxy thought to herself and strolled in confidently. Then, realizing that confidence might not match the visual, she dialed back the bravado. She still held her head high though.

As she moseyed along the pathway, she nodded and smiled at those who crossed her path. She received a few nods, a handful of smiles, and one "Good Morning." None of which could be considered as being legitimately hit on. She walked a couple of laps, stopping to sit at random benches. No one approached. *Maybe morning time is tougher for guys of substance,* Moxy thought to herself as she frowned. Onto Spot #3.

Usually Moxy did her grocery shopping on a just-in-time basis, choosing to hop into the organic food market on her way home after work. But, in an effort to be non-showy, she hit the Super BigBox, a combo supermarket/department store jammed to the gills with people. Upon entry, Moxy instantly deemed the place a chaotic, jumbled mess. She stood at the automatic sliding glass doors, debated about even going through with this spot. The chaos and noise rattled her nerves. Ultimately, she strengthened her resolve and entered.

Venturing inside Super BigBox was one thing. Touching a shopping cart was something else altogether. Moxy considered Chelsea a germaphobe and teased her to no end about it. But, when it came down to it, Moxy herself was just as cautious. Purchasing food using a shopping cart seemed uncouth and the mere thought of grasping onto those germ-ridden handles made her shudder. *I'll browse, buy a couple of things then go. I need tea anyways.* Moxy threaded through the aisles. This did not seem like a hot bed for romantic encounters, no pun intended and certainly no pun found. Lazily-dressed people pushed carts around and talked to each other loudly, dragging children who pleaded for toys and candy or anything within reaching range. Haggard parents obliged. There were some single guys there, but most looked tired and beaten by hard work or hard living. A couple of dudes glanced her way and gave impish grins but moved on. Moxy noticed one guy who made eye contact only to see him frown and hide the toilet paper he was holding behind his back. So much for this place. Onto Spot #4.

Angela's was popular with the locals and tourists alike. With amazing food and unparalleled ambiance, Angela's mixed the charm of an old world bistro with the minimalistic edge of a New York City design firm. The dining area was constructed in such a way to provide an al fresco experience regardless of the weather. On warm, sunny days, the patio section was open to the elements, sectioned off by a wall of pane glass with a door leading into the dining hall. When the weather was inclement, the entire patio area was enclosed using a motorized mechanism which unfolded glass panels in a dome over the diners. When mosquitoes and flies were rampant, a separate mechanized system enclosed the area with a screen. The setup must have cost a fortune, yet Angela's was always busy so the cost was warranted.

On that particular Saturday, the sun was shining and the weather was warm. All of Angela's patio was exposed to the brisk air. Moxy chose a table close to the sidewalk to make it easy for guys to notice her and make their approach. She had used this technique before at this very eatery and it never failed to generate interest.

Until now, that is.

Moxy felt as invisible here as she had felt at the coffeehouse. The staff was nice enough, but that was the extent of it. The feeling of being ignored and snubbed enraged her until she realized that all this was part of the experiment she had consciously created. At the same time, the results were leaning toward the conclusion that yes, she did in fact get more out of life in direct relation to her attractiveness.

The restaurant filled up fast. Adjacent to her table sat two college-aged guys. They were good looking and cocky. Moxy prepared herself for being approached by sitting up straight and projecting an *I love life* vibe.

After a few moments, she detected talk about her from the college guys. One said to the other, "Check her out. 'I'm a cheap date.' I guess you get what you pay for." They chuckled.

Moxy, now sure they were talking about her, faced them. "Are you making fun of my shirt?" she said in a slightly angry voice.

"Nah," returned one of the guys. "I'm making fun of *you* for wearing a shirt like that." He laughed at his own comment.

"You don't know anything about me," Moxy fumed. "What gives you the right to insult me?"

"It's a free country; freedom of speech," the guy retorted with a snicker. "If I think you look like a hobo librarian, I can say it. Are you gonna call the cops on me for having an opinion?"

Moxy glared at him.

"What's your story anyways?" He asked, now with a more serious tone. "You're a cute girl, but you're dressed like a bag lady."

"You don't know anything about me!" Moxy exclaimed again.

"You seem kinda bold for a bag lady. Most chicks like you don't give lip."

Moxy grew hot under her collar. "Give lip?" she asked angrily. "So you treat other girls like this and they just sit there and take it?"

"Yeah, basically."

Moxy's rage turned to curiosity. Why would other girls take crap from guys like this? Why would any girl subject herself to such abuse and not fight back? Her thoughts and memories bounced around in her head. She had known girls who took verbal abuse from their boyfriends, some of them had been friends of hers. It drove her crazy but she didn't interfere. She felt she didn't have the right. In addition, she told herself to not be nosy about the particulars of their relationship. To take abuse from a stranger, however, seemed out of bounds.

"Well, not this girl!" Moxy said curtly and turned away from him. She could hear the two guys making a few comments between themselves but she turned her ears off to them.

Other than the scuff with the college guys, she had no other interactions. That is until she heard a voice over her shoulder.

"Shouldn't a hobo librarian be reading a book or something?"

Startled, Moxy looked behind her. It was the faded brown jacket guy from the coffeehouse.

"Are you making fun of me too?" She said with a sneer. The guy chuckled.

"Calm down. I'm not making fun of you, just joshing you." The guy had a calm and inviting demeanor. He seemed slightly bookish with the air of intellectual confidence that is mistaken -- or not mistaken -- for pretentiousness. "Care for some company?"

Moxy didn't know what to make of it. Was this guy feeling pity for her? Is this a come on? What?

"Are you hitting on me?" She asked impertinently.

"If your objective is to get hit on, I'll leave. I have no interest in play-ing games."

"Games?" Moxy looked confused at the guy. He stood there silently. She picked up on his cues. "OK. Sit if you like." She feigned annoyance.

"Thank you." The guy sat across from her and leaned back in his chair. "Name's Moose. And you?"

"Moose?" Moxy let out a guffaw. The guy sat silently, unfazed.

"Oh," she said blushing. "You weren't kidding."

"I was not. My name is Moose." He paused. "I was born in Alaska. That's where my family still lives. I was birthed at the hands of a midwife in a pool in the living room of our family's home. The story goes like this: as I was being born, my dad looked out the window of our living room and there, staring in, was a bull moose. He saw it as a sign, spiritual… like a totem. So I was named after the creature."

"Ah." she felt small.

"And your name?"

"Moxy. I don't have a totem." She chuckled a bit nervously. Moose didn't chuckle but held his smile.

"Moxy," he said pointedly. "Got it."

Moxy couldn't decide if she thought he was good looking or not. He certainly wasn't her type. But then again, her type had failed her over and over again.

"Do you do this often? Just sit down and talk with some strange girl?"

"I don't know you well enough to deem you strange." He smiled broadly. She tried to be angry but couldn't help but smile along with him. He was humorous, that was for sure. And he had a way of softening the situation.

"I interact with people of all varieties whenever possible." He smiled. She blushed again. He seemed genuine and confident. Deep down she felt that, even if she was done up like normal, she still would have blushed.

"I see what you're doing," he said directly, "All this," he waved his open hand around Moxy's person, gesturing to the entirety of her.

"I don't know what you're talking about," she lied and sat straight and proud.

"The transformation. If I had to guess, I'd say you're doing a social experiment. Kudos."

Moxy crossed her arms and sat back in her chair. "What makes you say that?"

"You don't normally dress this way. I've seen you around, you're hard to miss. All dolled up and fancy." He looked her directly in the eyes. "Your face has certain features that are unmistakable. All faces do. I recognized you. Also, you're not comfortable in those clothes, ironically."

She picked up on the irony. "So you're onto me?"

"Yes. Tell me... why?"

"First you have to tell me if you are... *were* hitting on me."

"If you want to see it as that, sure."

Moxy was not satisfied with that answer. A definite *yes* or *no* would make this experience worth the effort.

"I am, in fact, doing an experiment," she said. "It's a vanity fast of sorts." She laid it all out for him. She shared with him her concern with her reliance on vanity, her newfound issues with feeling invisible, everything. Moose sat and listened attentively.

After Moxy had exhausted facts and feelings, Moose sat silent for a moment, taking it all in. Then he asked, "Will it change your lifestyle if you findings prove one way or another?"

"I haven't considered what I would do afterward." Her face tensed with thought. "I... well, I assumed I would go on like before."

"Then why, may I ask, do the experiment in the first place? If it doesn't matter, that is."

"You don't think it matters?"

"If it makes no difference in the trajectory of your life then no, it doesn't."

Moxy tried to wrap her brain around this statement. Did it make sense or not?

"What about you," she asked, shifting the focus to him. "What makes *you* tick?"

"Love."

"Are you some sort of playboy or something?"

"With all due respect, if you think love is encapsulated within sex, I feel sorry for you. Love is so much more than copulation."

Moxy felt sheepish and shallow. "Of course it is. I was just kidding."

Moose shrugged it off. "I love love. I love people. I love how people show each other love. Love is my passion." Moxy wanted to kid and say, *No pun intended,* but she knew better. This guy didn't seem to joke about this topic. He continued, "I used to be something of a playboy. You called it. I enjoy women, everything about them. I, for lack of a better term, in-dulged in as many women as possible. I am now able to admit that I was sick. I read up on ways to manipulate women -- the science of picking up chicks and all that. And it worked. Unfortunately, there are a lot of gullible women out there. In the end, I didn't want a gullible woman. I wanted a strong woman with a healthy mind and soul, deep within her own femininity. Not a headstrong woman, mind you. Just a strong woman to be my counterpart."

Moxy decided to probe. "And have you found such a woman?"

"I've found a few, no one that's compatible." A waiter came to the table. Moose said something to him discretely.

"So Moose, what exactly do you want from me?" Moxy questioned.

"Company."

"And then what?"

"I don't know. Maybe we can go find you a purple polka dot fur coat to go with your getup."

Moxy laughed.

"Actually, I think I'm cramping your style," he said. "You're wanting to get hit on and that's not going to happen as long as you're sitting with a *playboy*." He winked. She blushed again.

With that, Moose stood up and bid Moxy farewell. She wanted to talk to him more, hear more of his passionate speech. She especially liked how he listened to her; like he truly cared. She felt a strange longing for him. She sighed as he walked away.

Despite its density of diners, Angela's proved to be devoid of guys seeking romance. When she asked the waiter for her ticket, he told her it had been taken care of by her companion, tip and all. Moxy thought that was unnecessary yet classy. Here was a guy who didn't want anything more than to spend some time in her presence and he was willing to pick up the tab. She felt the longing again.

She went over her agenda. She still had the museum and art gallery, the mall and the wine and beer pub. However, her enthusiasm for the experiment was waning. All she could think about was Moose and his intensity within the moment; his sincerity and humor.

Something hit her. The experiment was about vanity and if our personalities shine through. For Moose, his personality was easy to detect yet his presence was unassuming and seemingly dull. When he spoke, he shined. Moxy pulled a compact from her purse and looked at herself in the mirror. Her appearance didn't match her personality. In some weird strange way, it was forced.

She realized that she would never get the answers she wanted because she wasn't being true to herself, at least not today. Even if a guy were to hit on her she would be something of a charlatan. The thought disgusted her even more than her previous thoughts on vanity.

She decided to abort the experiment. She would not find the answers at a museum or a mall or a pub. In fact, she felt like she had found her answer.

In her mind's eye, she saw Moose in his worn, faded brown coat. He was real. At the same time, she felt like he was a part of her imagination. Regardless, his presence lingered. She thought about her own personality and passions. Maybe her appearance was her passion. And if it was, so what? At least she had a passion. Whether her passion was noble or not, it was a strong part of her personality that could not be denied.

Moxy gathered her things and headed home. Once there, she stripped off the grubby clothes, underwear and all. She drew herself a bath and lined up her scented bath products. After a long hot bath, she engaged in her routine of making herself up. She loved the process and the end result.

It was 6:15 PM when she was properly prepared to hit the town. All she needed to do now was make a few calls to some friends to procure a clubbing companion for the night. She looked in the mirror at herself. Perfection. Any guy would be lucky to have her.

She looked over at the clothes from her experiment. They sat in a heap on her floor. She went to the kitchen and got a trash bag. She bagged all the clothes and threw them out. No need to take them for another round at the second-hand shop. Their purpose had been fulfilled.

As she got in her car, she felt a renewed sense of purpose. Maybe she wasn't deep. Maybe she didn't go on missions or help the poor or all that selfless stuff. But that wasn't her passion, at least not at this point in her life. Maybe all she had to offer was her beauty and charisma. Was that so wrong? In a world where people could be ugly and mean, perhaps pretty and nice may be deemed a valuable community.

Moxy turned on her car. *"Love is a Verb"* by John Mayer played over the speakers. The image of Moose flashed in her mind and her heart warmed. "I'll keep your words in my heart, Moose," she said aloud. Then, she turned up the radio and headed out on the town.

THE END

Prologue

The story I am about to share with you is screwed up and disturbing. It disturbed me immensely when Cal first told it to me; seems to disturb me more than him, as strange as that may sound. I have chosen to set aside my current writing project for the moment in order to share his story with you. It is, in my mind, a cautionary tale.

I recently ran into Cal on a Tuesday morning. I had made my way to the Argyle Café with full intention of downing multiple cups of coffee while pounding the keys on my next work. It was unseasonably warm for a September morning, especially in our neck of the woods. The air was no less brisk though. It was the perfect morning to catch up on my writing.

The café was alive with customers, much more than normal. I took my regular seat at the window bar and set up shop as I would any other day. The thing I love about this place is that Perk always notices me arrive and brings me my regular: a cup of half-caff black coffee heated through steaming to burning-tongue levels and served in a to-go cup. Perk and I exchanged brief pleasantries. He didn't linger though; the onslaught of customers seemed to have him and Compa in the weeds. I didn't mind. I had work to do.

I took a sip of coffee, pulled out my notes, opened my laptop, and began to type. As soon as I struck the first few keys, Cal ambled on in. In true charismatic form, he noticed me and strode right on up and gave a firm handshake. "Good morning, buddy!" He said, smiling confidently.

"Morning," I replied. "Where have you been? Haven't seen you for months, probably close to half a year." I set my work aside to talk with him, to catch up.

"Yeah, that sounds about right," he said. "I've gone dark for a while. I'm getting back into the swing of things."

"Any particular reason?"

"Yes. But I'm wary to share. It's a crazy story, juicy and strange. Life changing in a way. Horrifying too."

"Oh, really? What happened? Tell me."

"How much time do you have?"

"I've got some time." Sure, my work may have to wait but I figured this should be worth it.

"Alright. Let me get a cup of joe and I'll tell you. Save me a seat."

After a few minutes, he returned with a steaming mug of coffee. He sat beside me, took a swig and savored the moment. "I enjoy the little things so much more these days."

"Why is that?"

"I'll tell you but you're not going to believe it."

"Tell me."

"I'm serious. You're going to think I'm lying." He looked out the window. "Nice day isn't it. Sunshine and all." He was playing with me, making me want to hear his story.

"Come on, spit it out! You can't tell me you have some juicy story and then just sit there. It's torture!"

"Torture? You have no idea." He took another slow sip of coffee to build up my anticipation. I knew that for a fact due to the wink and the sly grin he gave me after he did it. I snickered and took a sip of my own brew.

"I haven't told anyone about this. I only tell you because, well, you and I go way back. I can trust you."

"Thanks."

He paused, looked to his left then to his right as if preparing to tell me his deepest, darkest secret. "Listen, dude. This is some serious stuff. Don't let on that you heard it. I'll deny everything."

"OK." (Note to reader: I only share it with you because, as I said, it's a cautionary tale and, of course, I can trust you.)

He proceeded to tell me the story that I will share with you in a moment. In all honesty, when I first heard it, I suspected that it was a fib; an engaging yarn that he was spinning as some sort of writing experiment. That is until, after my incessant requests, he exposed his proof to me in the privacy of the café's mens room. I saw it with my own eyes.

Looked like it must have hurt. After reading, you'll know this proof that I speak of. The following account is written as close to his original story as possible and in his vernacular, as far as I can remember. It is slightly altered from his telling as I had to: 1) recount it from memory, and 2) format it for easier reading. For obvious reasons, I excluded formalities, interruptions by the café staff, and an instance where Cal briefly engaged an attractive woman passing by. Outside of that, it's all here.

Just a warning, the story does contain some elements of, how shall I refer to it… gore. I've even toned down some of his description for the sake of those with a fragile disposition.

On a lighter note, I'm writing this introduction after transcribing his accounting of the occurrence. That means that I have been able to get back to my initial project. I'm very excited about it and I know you will be as well. Until then, however, I hope the story on the pages that follow give you some insight; not just into Cal's nature, but into the nature of a psycho chick.

And, as always, thank you for reading.

Jason Salas

Could something as innocent as a wink and a smile get a guy killed? Well, that's what happened to me. Almost. I'm still alive to tell the tale, yet not unscathed.

It was roughly six months ago. I got myself tangled up with a psycho chick, not your run of the mill stalk-you-and-scream-at-you psycho chick, this chick was legitimately psycho; certifiable. I'll tell you what happened as I remember it happening.

I woke up, flat on my back, in a strange bed. I had no idea where I was. I went to rub my eyes and couldn't move. My wrists and ankles were bound tightly to the bed posts with thick zip ties, several of them on each wrist and ankle. I was sprawled out like an "X." I immediately became alert. I remember saying, 'What the…" and quickly shutting my mouth. Whoever it was that tied me up might hear me and realize I was awake. I did not remember anything from the night before. Can you believe that? Me, Cal Stout, the guy who always has a plan and a back up plan when it comes to girls. And I was lost as to the particulars of my situation. And while I've played games like this before, this didn't seem like a game. I have never been zip tied nor was I ever left alone and unconscious. That's messed up. You just don't do that to someone.

I looked down and saw that I was stripped down to my underwear. *At least I'm not completely naked,* I assured myself then instantly thought, *my junk!* Memories of horror stories from the media swam through my mind -- stories of angry women with knives. Yet I wasn't in any sort of pain and saw no blood, so that was a plus. I kind of wiggled and, yeah, the boys downstairs were still residing.

I was in a room filled with natural light. I scanned my surroundings and noticed that the decor was neither masculine nor feminine; bare walls and indiscriminate furnishings amid what appeared to be loads of women's clothing strewn about everywhere. The accurate description would be to say that the room was *infested* with women's clothing -- piles of warm-up gear in neon green and black or neon pink and black, yoga pants by the dozen, frilly bras strewn haphazardly and hanging from various fixtures, socks, shoes, everything. That alone was torture. I mean, you know me. I'm all about simple, clean, and uncluttered. But somehow I knew that laziness may be the least of this chick's personality flaws. The smell of patchouli was thick but it didn't completely mask the pungent scent of body odor. Whoever this girl was, she worked out hard, and didn't do her laundry. Not the kind of girl who has many visitors. I know myself and I would not have stayed in such a room. I would have turned tail and ran. This made the question of how I got there even more mysterious.

To my right was a window with light-colored semi-transparent drapery, thicker opaque drapery pulled to the side to let light in. I could make out leaves but nothing more, like the side of the top of a mature tree. I was on the second floor from what I could tell. The window was weathered wood and open about an inch or so, looked like it was painted open and wouldn't shut. There was a slight breeze ruffling the sheer drapery cloth. It was raining. Not much, but enough so that I could hear raindrops gently tap upon the leaves. The sound was surprisingly calming to me. It was a welcome relief -- albeit a small relief -- from the precariousness of the situation.

There were two doors in the room. One was the closet, open like a gaping wound bleeding lady clothes from its gash. That meant the other door was the entry door. It was shut and on the back of it was a poster of an abnormally fit woman in a workout bra and bloomers. The words, *"Take Back Your Life!"* were printed in large bold letters across the top. Gaudy.

"I'd love to take back my life, lady," I said softly, chuckling at the appropriateness of the message. The moment faded and reality set in again. *Where was I last night? What day is it?*

The only thing I could recall was a cab. This made absolutely no sense whatsoever since I make it a point to drive myself to wherever I'm going. And I hate cabs; too dirty, too expensive. Could I have been drunk? No. I haven't broken my five drink limit in forever, plus I didn't remember having more than two, maybe three drinks.

And while I never take cabs, I couldn't be sure I didn't last night. After all, I was not in control at that moment, who's to say I wasn't in control during some cab ride? I was racking my brain with no headway so I decided to reach back further into my memory and walk forward.

The café.

I stopped by the Argyle Café earlier that afternoon. Perk had asked to borrow a book and I was dropping it off and grabbing a bite. The food isn't the best on earth but, if Compa was in a good mood, he might hook me up with a double serving.

A double serving.

I remember bribing Compa into giving me a double serving and to make it quick because I was in a rush. I used photographs as currency. It was from a catalog in which I was hired to write copy; descriptions of each item. The company sold hemp clothing for women. I thought Compa would like some pics from the undergarment section. There were two that I presented as payment: one was of a college-aged girl in matching hemp bra and panties. The set was made to look like pot leaves. The girl was not gorgeous but thin and angular with long straight hair. Kind of weird looking but I know Compa is a sucker for girls with long straight hair. The second pic had a buxom blonde in a tight fitting underwear ensemble. The bra and panties were knitted with hemp yarn. This made the garments sheer. I had hoped these pics might land me a fat sandwich, maybe even for free. But why so much food? And why in a rush? A rush to...

The cabin.

Fragments in my memory started to align. I was going to a cabin in Lakewood, a small rural community outside of town, just inside the forest area at the cusp of the mountains. I needed the extra food because the drive took 45 minutes and I didn't know how long I would be out there. I wanted to have some food I trusted instead of searching for some backwards greasy spoon.

I'm laying there trying to remember all this stuff then it hit me, why was I wasting time trying to figure it out? I should get free then analyze later. I inspected my wrists and the zip ties that bound them. The bedposts were made of wood. The zip ties were secured snugly under a spherical knob on each bed post. I rotated my wrist in an attempt to grab the knob, unscrew it if it allowed. The ties were too tight and the sharp edges sliced the skin on my wrists as I struggled and I could feel the blood dripping down my arm. Nothing deep, but stinging nonetheless. I kept at it though, figured those wounds might pale in comparison to the unknown wounds that might be awaiting me. But for all my twisting and grabbing, I couldn't free myself. My captor had done too good of a job. It looked like three or four zip ties on each limb. Fat ones too. She really didn't want me going anywhere.

I laid there silently, keeping my ear tuned to potential noises from the other parts of the house. Nothing. I looked for an alarm clock for the time. None. I looked for a picture, anything to give me some sort of clue. Aside from the poster on the door, there was nothing. If there was anything like that, it was shrouded by the layers of crap. I gave a few more strong tugs at my wrists, all in vain, then figured it might be best to let my brain get back to work.

Why a cabin? Why the rush? The thought repeated itself in my mind. It wasn't for recreation, I remembered that much. If it were, I wouldn't have worried about the duration. When I'm someplace and I want to leave, I leave. Simple as that. So the cabin must have been for work. That thought was now repeating itself in my mind. *For work... for work...*

The memories were not coming as easily. All I saw was fog, an abyss in my mind. Sure, I thought about calling for help but thought better of it based on two things. The first reason was that I was safe for the time being. Calling for help might set off the psycho chick. By the way, that's how I referred to her in my mind: the *Psycho Chick*. Seemed reptilian-like, which was the feeling I got from her at that point. The second reason was that I wasn't sure that the situation wasn't entirely dangerous. Yet, I don't do the S&M bit so I ruled reason number two out, thus leaving reason number one. Thus leaving me with the decision to keep quiet.

I kept thinking *cabin, rush, work... cabin, rush, work.* I shut my eyes tight which amplified the dull ache in my head. Not good. Maybe I was hit, or drugged or both. *Cabin, rush, work... Cabin, rush, work... Concert!*

That was the connection. There was a concert at the cabin. It was starting to come back. In fact, the event was called *"Concert at The Cabin."* The Cabin is a house in which the owners host concerts featuring traveling musicians. I was hired by a local arts and entertainment magazine to attend the concert and interview the performer. I was running late, hence the rush. *Rush...* Oh, yeah. A memory surfaced, flashing cop car lights in my rear view mirror coupled with that sinking feeling in my gut. Then the cop, a lady cop. I remember that for sure. Her facial features and our interaction started to materialize. "Why the big hurry, big guy?" The lady cop was speaking authoritatively yet politely. And did I detect a hint of flirtation in her tone?

"I'm trying to get to an assignment, ma'am. I'm a writer, reviewing a concert at The Cabin and I'm cutting it close." I remembered her lips, she pulled them into a slight tense pucker as if she was either imitating a cop from a TV show or perhaps she was just as intense as the dramas made cops out to be. Her nose was straight and dimpled at the end. Cute. She wore reflective aviator sunglasses which I thought was a touch of 80's class and unabashed irony. Besides the fact that she was making me late for my gig, I liked her. "That's the truth, ma'am," I told her, trying to lay on some charm to get out of a ticket and, more importantly, get to the show. Her name tag read "Perez." Latina. I liked that too.

"You were going twenty miles per hour over the speed limit," she said curtly. "Now *that's* the truth." She removed her sunglasses with gusto, also like the TV cops, and revealed a set of eyes like topaz jewels, amber and bright. I'm a sucker for a chick with amber eyes. She suppressed a grin and tried working the intense look. I could tell she was being playful or not. "Listen," she continued, "I'll let you off with a warning but you're going to have to promise me you'll drive slower."

"You got it."

"Here's my card. That's my cell phone number. I'll need for you to call me to let me know you're keeping your promise. Comprende?" She allowed a hint of smile peek out from behind her mock stern facade. Then she winked at me. Double score. I got out of a ticket and got her number in the process.

"Loud and clear, Officer Perez." I mimicked her false intensity, hiding my own smile. "If I don't, you will have no choice but to put me in handcuffs."

She giggled at that, couldn't hold it in. Then she donned her fake intense expression again, put her sunglasses back on and said, "Sounds like a deal. Now beat it!"

The interaction was amusing despite the current predicament. I hoped I still had that card in my pocket somewhere. Wouldn't mind a ride along with Officer Perez. The handcuffs thing I could do without, especially with the zip ties eating into my arms.

The interaction with Officer Perez jogged my memory about the drive the rest of the way out to The Cabin. I obeyed the speed limit, I didn't want to get pulled over again. Why press my luck? I remembered arriving at the venue amid a small crowd of people. I couldn't quite remember the performer's name. It was a woman. Irrelevant. That is, unless the woman was in the other room. No. She was a traveling performer and just alright, nothing memorable. At least not now. Sure hope my notes were good because whatever was going on in my mind, was making everything cloudy.

Cloudy... rain.

It was raining and... My Jeep! I could remember approaching my Jeep as I got ready to leave and finding out I had two flats and only one spare. There was a woman too, couldn't remember her face. It was dark. That must have been why I took a cab. But that's when things started to get blurry. The only thing I could remember after that was texting someone, probably about my ride. But even that was like a black hole and no amount of straining could conjure up any more memories. That was it. I had nothing more. I was hamstrung physically and mentally. Pretty bleak.

A door slammed in the other room; a big door, possibly the front door. I heard clicks of footsteps move about along with the rustle of bags. "Hey," I called out. Obviously whoever was out there knew I was inside and was going to get to me eventually. And if it wasn't the Psycho Chick, maybe they would help.

The footsteps stopped then picked up again, heading toward the room and stopping at the closed door. The doorknob turned slowly and made a thunk as the door freed itself from the jamb. It opened at an even slower rate than the turning of the doorknob. Whoever it was -- most likely the Psycho Chick -- had a flair for the overly dramatic.

The door opened inward but only halfway; it's opening was opposite from the light coming through the window, no light was cast on the person behind it. Still, I could see the outline of a woman, darker against the dull darkness deep in the room behind her. The drapes on the windows in the front rooms must have been pulled shut to keep the outside light out during the day or the inside light in during night or both. Why did she leave the drapes open in her bedroom? Illogical behavior, especially with me, her captive, in here. "Hey," I called again. "Cut these things off of me, will ya? This is not fun!"

The door swayed slightly on its hinges, the person -- a woman -- on the other side was chuckling. It was a strange breathy laugh that crescendoed into a cackle like a harpy. For sure this was the Psycho Chick. "Oh, I will," she said in a shrill voice. "I will most certainly cut *them* off!" the Psycho Chick cackled again and closed the door as slowly and creepy as she had opened it.

She's going to cut my balls off, I thought to myself. *Dammit!*

The footsteps clicked away into the other room. I felt myself getting angry. I was no closer to figuring out what was happening.

I thought *What would Steve McQueen do?* I pictured McQueen on his motorcycle escaping prison. That would work if I had a crew and a bike. Not so much for a half naked dude tied up with no co-conspirators. The Psycho Chick was humming something out of tune. It was horrible. I hated her voice, yet there was something familiar about her cackle. Maybe a witch from a movie or something. So much for my great escape.

I worked at the bedpost knob again, in spite of the stupid zip ties eating me up. My left hand gained purchase on the knob and I tried unscrewing it. It wouldn't budge. I tried my right hand. Same thing. Probably glued on. I heard the Psycho Chick return to the room and stand outside the closed door once again.

She did her silly little routine of opening up the door all slow and creepy. The bit was already stale. This time, however, the door opened completely to reveal the Psycho Chick in all her not-so-captivating glory. She was thin, fit, and trim. She wore a tight t-shirt which accentuated her all-too-fake round breasts. She wore yoga pants and I could see her muscular shape beneath her clothes. She wasn't overly muscular like a bodybuilder but impressive nonetheless, I had to admit; tight and taught. And orange. She was so orange it was sickening. She looked like a carrot, tanned to imperfection.

She had a mass of curly hair that shadowed her face. I squinted, trying to make out some features but she kept them hidden. "I have a plan for you," she said and held up a tote bag that said *"ShakeFit"* on it. I thought it was comical that she was threatening me with a tote bag from an multi-level marketing company. She could have used a brown paper bag or a suitcase, but whatever. She rattled the bag's contents. It sounded like kitchen utensils. "I'm taking my life back!" She cackled her harpy laugh again. I cringed, not so much out of fear, but out of disgust. Yuck!

"I saw the poster," I returned with a half smile. I couldn't help it. Inside I knew for certain that I didn't want to get castrated by this lunatic, yet why show her any fear? Why give her the satisfaction? Especially when I had no idea what she had against me.

"Oh, you're *sooo* charming all the time, aren't you?" Her tone was overly sarcastic to hyperbolic proportions. She approached me, revealing her face. She had tight, angular features, almost inhuman and doll-like. Her nose was defined and small. Her chin, square and petite, her cheekbones overly pronounced. She wore too much make up for my liking, the foundation not matching the orange of the rest of her body. She was what I call a *barroom bruja,* the kind of woman who might charm you in a dark barroom but, when you see her in the daylight, you wonder what sort of spell she had cast on you. "You don't remember last night, do you." She said it more as a statement than a question.

"No."

"Good. But you'll remember today. At least until it's over, then you won't remember anything. You'll be…": She reached into her tote bag and shuffled her hand around theatrically.

"Shaken? Stirred?" I couldn't help it.

"No… Dead!" She jerked her hand out of the bag, revealing a bread knife. She smiled menacingly, baring glowing white teeth.

"That's a bread knife. You know that, right?"

"It slices, it dices!" She licked her lips, which confused me to no end. Was she a cannibal?

"Bread knives don't dice. They're made for slicing only." It was dangerous ground, playing with her that way. I had no leverage. Still, I was frustrated and angry with her and felt justified in pointing out her ineptitude.

"I know that, jerk!" Her head cocked back with every syllable. She looked like some absurd bird wearing a wig. "I was making a ha-ha."

A *ha-ha?* Who says that?

"Pardon me for not laughing. I'm not in the mood for jokes."

"Well I'm not in the mood for you being such a pompous, chauvinistic pig!"

"Having experience with kitchen utensils would make me *less* of a chauvinist, wouldn't you say so?"

The Psycho Chick didn't respond. She laid her bread knife on her dresser then rummaged through her bag again. "OK, smart guy, then what is *this?*" She pulled out a round plastic object.

"I can't see it," I said politely. "Bring it closer."

Strangely, she obliged. She instantly switched to a servile nature and approached me, almost like a friend. I evaluated the object. "It's an egg slicer for hard-boiled eggs." She looked at it confused.

"Really?" She said sheepishly.

"Yeah. You put the egg on those metal wires then press the top down," I said as I watched her move the object over and over in her hand like a curious chimpanzee holding a mysteriously foreign object.

"Wouldn't the shell get all in the egg?"

"You remove the shell before using it. If you boil an egg, I'll show you how it works. You'll have to untie me though."

"Never!" She pulled the egg slicer to her chest.

It seemed as though she let her curiosity take place of her rage but snapped back into evil mode at my request for freedom. "You think I'm stupid but you're the stupid one, stupid!" An adequately stupid comeback. "I don't care what this thing does to eggs," she seethed, "all I care about is what it will do to *you!*" She shoved the egg slicer back into the bag and felt around. She pulled out a large wooden slotted spoon."Now, lets get started, shall we?" The woman set her bag down on a pile of clothes. I didn't know what to expect but it wasn't straining pasta, that much was for sure.

She turned the spoon over and struck me in the knee with the handle end. The spoon and my kneecap made a high-pitched knock. "Ow!" I yelped. "Are you insane?" I wriggled about. The blow stung but wore off quickly. I'm no stranger to the pain of being hit. I trained with some mixed martial arts guys. Never fought in the ring, but I did a ton of sparring and grappling. What got me was that I was defenseless. And the Psycho Chick seemed to have bigger plans than just smacking me around with a wooden spoon.

"Me? Insane? Oh, that's rich! Especially coming from you!" She sneered with her neon white teeth and smacked me again. This time I refused to react. "Tough guy, eh?" She turned the spoon around and held it by its handle. Then she conked me on the head with it. What brand of torture was this? Vaudevillian?

"Why are you doing this? Who the hell are you?" I glared at her right in the eyes. She had a slight case of wall eye which made her seem distant and detached like she was staring through me. I softened my tone. "Let me start. My name is Cal. What is your name?" I gave her a grin and raised my eyebrows. It was the same look I give to younger girls -- a look that says, *I'm a grown up, and you're a child.* Condescending? Sure. But I developed that tactic to place a divide between me and underage girls who may get the wrong idea. That has happened, more than once.

"I know who you are! I've known you for years!"

"Years?"

"Yes, years!"

"Listen, I don't know you at all and I don't even remember meeting you last night. I assume we met last night."

She turned the wooden spoon in her hand. "We didn't meet last night but we were…" She looked down her nose at me, "together."

"I don't know. You're not my type."

"Oh no? Not your type? Firm, fit, pretty. Isn't that your *only* type?"

"A lot of girls fit that description, and I've dated my fair share. But there's something about you that rubs me the wrong way. Maybe it's because you want to cut me up with a bread knife. I don't know."

She threw the wooden spoon across the room and dug in her tote bag. This time she remove a paring knife, short and worn with a white plastic handle. I shifted a bit. The situation just got real. It may not be the biggest knife but it would cut all the same.

She held up the blade between her eyes and said slowly, "You're going to want to lay still for this." She jumped on top of me from the side, like getting up onto a horse, straddling me at the waist. She inched the knife close to my face, humming that horrendous tune the whole time. I could smell her pungent odor, like her discarded clothes but now emitting directly from the source, radiating off. I turned my head away from her. She sat up and positioned the knife over my right pec and began cutting into skin with short, sketchy movements. I couldn't believe it. I jerked roughly. "Stay still," she demanded. I pulled at my wrists again, trying to pry my hands free. The cuts on my chest were not deep but not shallow either. It was all I could do to keep from screaming as the knife scratched jaggedly across my skin. The metal felt foreign and wicked, the pain intense. Blood freely flowed out. I tried to buck her off of me but I couldn't get enough oomph being tied up so tight. She frowned at me then went back to work. The sting of the new wounds mixed with the raw pulsing pain of the cuts she just made. I resolved to keep a straight face even though I probably winced a lot more than I would have liked; shown my fear and pain. She was writing something. I looked down but couldn't make out what it was. Blood was everywhere. It was nasty. And *she* was nasty, just carving into me like it was no big deal. There was little I could do so I just laid there and thought I might as well figure out who she was. Maybe a little conversation might buy me some time, maybe even get her to like me somehow. Possibly work out a negotiation.

"You said you know me," I said calmly, "but I don't know you."

"Yes you do," she returned.

"No I don't."

"Yes you *do!* You just don't *remember* me. And you don't *recognize* me. Not now. Not after my glorious transformation." She held her arms out and flicked her hair.

"Transformation?"

"Yes. The work of art you see before you now is not the person you met all those years ago. My name is Ginny. At least that's what I go by. You won't remember me by that name."

"I don't remember you by any name."

"Shut up!" With that Ginny slapped me hard across my face. My blood began to boil but I kept my cool. No sense in riling up a crazy lady with a knife.

"I'm sorry," I said softly taking the honey-rather-than-vinegar approach. "What name would I have known you by?"

"Deana."

Deana... Deana.. I accessed my memory banks. Did I wrong a Deana? I've been less than a gentleman with many girls but few of them have I outright wronged. "Have we ever… you know?" I winked at her and instantly regretted it. This woman wanted to kill me and I was trying to charm her. Idiot.

"No. But I would have, you know? Even back then." Ginny instantly looked somber and sad. She had stopped carving around mid left pec. The sheer weight of each emotion pressed heavily upon her, swinging her from emotion to emotion. I have dated women who were bipolar but none were violent. Some had stalked me but never targeted me in criminal way. I sensed Ginny may have some of that bipolar thing going on inside. She was definitely not one hundred percent there. It seemed more serious than just bipolar. It was an imbalance for sure but I'm not a doctor so I couldn't say for sure.

I gave her a moment, not saying anything. Obviously she was troubled and whatever I had done had brewed inside her for a long time. Finally I broke the silence and said, "Listen, I'm really confused and uncomfortable. And you carving a message into my chest doesn't help. But this can't be about me, right?" I softened my face to her, raising my eyebrows, trying to look pathetic. She looked me in the eyes. She was crying. "I admit I don't remember you and that probably makes me a tool, but if you're going to do this -- going to kill me --" I paused. Saying it made it even that much more real. "If you are going to end my life, and end your life too since they will catch you, then I feel I deserve to know once and for all what this is all about."

Her face puckered in anger then she relaxed. I could tell the gears were turning in her head but wondered how much sand was gumming up the works. "You said you loved me!" Ginny hissed and got back to carving at my chest. I winced at her tone and, of course, the cutting. "You said you would always love me!"

"When did I say that?" I was honestly curious. I never tell girls I love them, and especially not girls like Ginny.

"You came to my high school. It was for a career day thing, your table was journalism. We talked for a while. I looked…" she paused, "*different* then. I was chubby and I had glasses and braces. I wrote poetry and I talked to you about writing. You were so handsome and confident and you were flirting with me." She clutched her hands to her chest, bloody knife and all, and looked painfully at me.

"Wait. Flirting? If I was at a high school for a career day, I was *not* flirting. I don't do that."

"But you *were!*" Ginny nearly screamed it. "You even winked at me!"

I didn't remember that particular interaction but I have to admit I do wink at a lot of people: women, men, kids, the elderly, everyone.

"When I had to go," Ginny continued, returning to her painfully sad face and tone yet still carving, "I asked if I could talk more about journalism with you. You told me to get back to you after I graduated high school. Then you said, 'But until then, know this, I will always love you.'"

That was it. She had me. Yes, I probably did say that. In fact, there was a time in my life when I told everyone that. Yet I said it in a jesting, overly dramatic manner. Stupid me. Ginny must not have caught on. I've come to realize that some high school girls are on their own island of reality.

Ginny went on, "I couldn't wait to see you after graduation. I was so nervous to call you. I knew you were the one for me because you loved me even though none of the other boys would even talk to me." Cal started putting the pieces together. She continued, "I wanted to see you." She began to sob slightly. "I tried to call the number from your business card but it didn't work. And you weren't in the phone book and your website didn't have your number either. Not even an email address."

That checked out as I've changed my number a few times on account of those aforementioned stalkers. These days I do most of my business via an email address which I hold close to my chest. I only phone from an online account if absolutely necessary.

"Then I found you," Ginny said, no sob in her voice but anger again. "You were at a restaurant with… some floozy!" I knew what was coming. I remembered the incident before she could get it out. "I went up to you and let you have it! I told you how you said you loved me and how dare you go out with other girls when you told me you loved *me*. What was I? Some high school fling for you?"

That was a horrible memory. The girl was batty and enraged. The whole place was looking at me like I was a pervert. I called for security to have her removed. I could do that sort of thing at that particular restaurant. Being a regular patron, they knew me well. I was, in my mind, honestly innocent of any wrongdoing. And this girl was bat crap, throwing stuff and yelling. She even tossed wine in my face and my date's face. It was a disaster.

Ginny growled through her teeth, "You had me kicked out of there and I didn't do anything wrong! *You* were the one coming on to a high schooler and denying it all! And I know why: it's because you thought I was ugly compared to your precious little girlfriend. That slut!"

The whole thing seemed ridiculous and way out of proportion.

"Guys like you are scum!" She said pulling her face close to mine, "and I'm ridding the earth of scum like you, one by one!" She pulled back. "The only reason you talked to me last night was because I look like this." She smiled and mimicked the pose of the girl in the poster.

As she said it, I remembered talking to her, indirectly. At one point in the night, I was talking to another person and a girl came up beside me and asked what I was drinking. Not looking at her, I answered that I was enjoying a glass of merlot. She had said something like, "Wine makes me so giddy!" Then laughed that her absurd laugh. That's why I remembered her cackle. It was from the concert. I didn't, however, remember spending any time with her. In fact, I made it a point to not even look in her direction. If I *had* looked at her, I probably would have striven even harder to avoid her. That must have been her though, at the end of the night outside by my Jeep. She must have drugged me somehow. Can't remember with what or how. Damn her!

It seemed like she had finished the message she had been cutting into my chest. She sat back and admired her handiwork and smiled. Then she reverted back into her intensity. "I've been working on myself for the last three years, making myself gorgeous so that one day, when we met again, I could do this."

"Ginny, It's a --"

"Shut up! After I get rid of you, I'm going to get rid of all the other guys like you. Yeah! Lure them in and put them down. I'm like a..." She looked to the ceiling as if she was searching for the right word. "A black widow! Or a *tan* widow! Yeah, that's me! The Tan Widow! Defender of girls from the scum of the earth! Maybe I'll even get a special suit made." As ludicrous as the whole situation was, I realized that this girl was a serious threat, not just to myself but potentially to other people and most certainly to herself.

Ginny dismounted me and shuffled to the kitchen. I could hear her rummaging through utensils and humming to herself.

A rustling come from outside the window. To my surprise, a head popped up slowly. At this point, I though I must have been having a nightmare and this was when the aliens entered the scene. But the head had hair and, shiny reflective sunglasses. It was Officer Perez! I was elated to see her; thought I might get out alive after all. I whispered, "Hey!" Her whole face came into view and she put her finger to her lips in a *shhh* manner then mouthed the question, "Where is she?"

"Kitchen," I mouthed back. Then, in a loud whisper, "She's going to kill me!"

Perez shushed me again and mouthed the words, "I know." That didn't seem too encouraging. Her face slowly moved down and out of sight as she descended what must have been a ladder.

"Hurry!" I said as soft as I could manage, trying to let my voice fall below Ginny's radar.

"What did you say?" Ginny called from the kitchen. "Hurry? You're excited to die? You really *are* sick! But I won't be quick about it. I'm going to cut you to pieces. Maybe I'll start with your--"

"Hurry!" I called out louder.

"Hold your horses, lover boy," Ginny came back into the room with a long thin razor-sharp knife. "This is a fillet knife, Mr. Know-it-all. It's for cutting meat!" Her smile was evil. Then she ran to the bed and jumped onto me as she had done before, straddling my stomach. I flinched. "I'm going slice you up slowly just like I did to Dave!"

Dave? So she had done this before? What did Dave do to deserve this?

Ginny pulled my left ear away from my head. "Now don't move. You'll only make it worse." She drew the knife to the top of my ear slowly and started to slice downward. Oh, I lost it. I cried out, "Ahhhr-rr!" Sure, I told myself I didn't want to give her the satisfaction of hearing me yelp in pain but now that she was actually cutting pieces off of me, I couldn't refrain. I wanted to jerk my head away but I didn't know what she would do with the knife if I did, or if it would tear my ear off.

Just then a loud crack came from the front room and a voice yelled out, "Police! Come out with your hands up! We know you're in there, Virginia!" It was a man's voice, not Officer Perez's. Ginny seized up. Her pupils contracted to a pinpoint and she exposed her teeth like an angry dog. "Come out, Virginia! You don't want us to go in there after you! It won't be pretty!" I felt like saying, *It already ain't pretty,* but it was not the time for jokes.

Ginny yelled over her shoulder, "I'm not going to come out until my work here is done!" Then she directed her attention back to me. "Now where were we?" She continued to slice down on my ear. "I didn't cut Dave's ear off. This is easier than I thought. No bones. Bones are tough to cut through. Have to use a saw." She was now in a trance, completely oblivious to the police outside her door. Or in denial.

"Virginia!" The voice was now a woman's voice. "If you do not come out with your hands up, we will have no choice but to go in there." I'm smart enough to realize that I wasn't out of the woods just yet. If Ginny was smart, she would hold me hostage, possibly inflict damage to me in a stand-off.

"I'm on the ears right now," Ginny said, almost amicably. "I've got a lot of work to do. He's a big guy. It might take me a while to get him all chopped up. Go ahead and come back in a few hours." Ginny was now in a far off place, completely detached from reality. Sucked to be me at that point.

I heard the front door bust open followed by murmurs, then a rumble of feet as the police made their way to the bedroom. Ginny was not affected in the least. "Freeze! Put the knife down!" There were two police officers in the doorway, Officer Perez and a man, a plain clothes officer. Didn't look like anyone else was with them. Ginny kept slicing downward. She was slow and uneven, about a one fourth of the way down from what I could feel. I could feel the blood streaming down the side of my head. The cut stung fiercely.

"We mean it, Virginia! Put the knife down and step away from him with your hands up!" Ginny simply hummed her tune and kept slicing. "If you don't put the knife down, we will have to apprehend you any way possible. Do you understand, Virginia? In any way possible!" Ginny kept slicing slowly, felt like she was now about half way down my ear.

Suddenly there was a thunk and Ginny's face spasmed strangely then she fell down on me in a slump, unconscious. Perez was standing there holding a black baton. "Wow, that was easy," she exclaimed, satisfied.

"Get her off of me!" I demanded. "And be careful, the knife's still in my ear!"

I felt the weight of Ginny lighten as the officers pulled her body off of mine. I heard the snap of handcuffs, Ginny being confined. The male officer got up and left the room saying something about the med kit. Perez stepped up and looked down at me. "Lover boy?" she said with a smirk.

"What?"

"It's carved on your chest." Perez couldn't help but grin. "Why does that not surprise me?"

"Untie me, will ya?" With the situation under control, I was no longer angry nor anxious. Of course I wanted my ear tended to but the other officer was on the case. Perez called out to the other guy to bring a pair of snips to cut the zip ties. She sighed and, with a grin said, "I love this job."

The sound of sirens and approaching vehicles filled the air. In a moment, the other officer returned and was followed in by more police officers and paramedics. Possibly a fireman or two.

Perez switched to full professional policewoman mode and cut loose my wrists and ankles, all the while telling me what to expect from the situation. She handed me a gauze of sorts and told me to hold it on my dangling ear. "You're lucky," Perez said to me. "We believe this woman has done this before." Ginny was still unconscious and the medics were tending to her, checking her vital signs.

"Dave?" I asked.

"Yes. What did she tell you?"

"Do I need a lawyer? This seems serious."

"You're the victim here, Cal. If you know anything about the whereabouts of the other victim, Dave -- David, that is. David Richardson -- you'll need to tell us."

"She said she cut him up. Mentioned something about how it was tough to cut through the bones. That's all I know."

Perez quickly stood up and whispered something to the plain clothes cop. He addressed the room. "We're upping this scene to possible homicide. There may be a body stashed somewhere." There was a lot of cop talk and people moving around. I just wanted to leave.

A paramedic hovered over me, tending to my cuts and ear. He informed me that I would need further medical attention. Perez came back to my side. I asked, "Is there any way possible I could get dressed and out of this God forsaken place?"

"Yes, of course. You'll have to go to the hospital and get proper medical attention. That ear will need to be surgically reattached. It's not as easy as just sewing it back on. There are blood vessels and all that. You leave it like that and it might rot off or heal just hanging there." Nasty, I know. "We'll need an official statement from you but we can do that after you have been seen by a doctor."

She found my clothes. I checked my pockets to make sure all my stuff was there. Everything was there except my phone. Apparently Psycho Chick had no use for wallet and keys. But my phone? I looked around briefly but didn't see my phone anywhere. No big deal. It's secured with a pass code and I had an app that would allow me to find it from my laptop. I got dressed and did my best not to disturb the mess that was Ginny's room and house. After all, if Ginny had done this before, anything could be evidence. Perez led me out of the front door and down the stairs onto the front porch. Ginny lived in the upper level of a house, modified into a duplex. The police had worked quickly to section off the house and the street in front. Onlookers were gawking.

Perez said something to the paramedic then sat me down on a deck chair on the porch, she remained standing. "They'll give you a ride to the emergency room. I told them to give us a second." She paused. "You don't seem too shaken up."

"It's weird," I said. "the whole thing seemed like some big joke until she started carving me up. Could be worse though. For a second I thought she was going to go after my… ahem, not my ear." Perez chuckled. I told her, "You don't seem too rattled either. Do you see this sort of thing often?"

"Not like this. We get domestic calls but those are more fights and what not. This was a premeditated deal and a detective -- the plain-clothes cop that came in with me -- was already on the Richardson case. I got your text, that's the only reason we found you."

"My text?"

"Yeah. You texted me last night, kind of late. You said you thought you had been drugged and couldn't talk and that you might be in trouble with some *psycho chick,* your words, not mine. But that was all you said. I instantly got a hold of the detective, thought this might be related somehow. We had no way of knowing where you went until we called up the cab companies and found the one that you and her used. The driver said he helped a drunk couple home, said he had to lug a big white guy up the stairs into the apartment."

"It took you until morning to figure out where I was at, even with the cab driver?"

"All we had to go off of was your text. But you didn't state your name so I didn't know who you were. I attempted to cross-reference your number with our databases but nothing came up. You must have changed your number since getting your license." I had, of course for all the reasons I mentioned earlier. "I called you back, texted too. No response. And your voice mail didn't state your name. Could have been anyone. We had to find some way of getting your identity first -- we pulled your phone records."

"Doesn't my phone have a GPS chip or something?"

"It does. Didn't help us. Well, actually it did help us. Ginny dumped your phone in a dumpster behind a fast food joint. We were able to hack into your phone and identify you as its owner. I recognized your name as well as your face from your pictures. Lover boy indeed." She gave me a wink and a slight smile then continued, "I remember you saying you had an assignment at The Cabin. Luckily I know about the place. I had been there not so long ago, noise complaint from the neighbors. The woman there said she saw you looking drunk and get into a cab with a woman. I saw your Jeep there with a couple flats too. That's when we got a hold of the cab driver."

"Oh. Guess I should have stated my name."

"Would have sped the process along." She smiled. "We had no idea about Virginia though, Deana I mean. She uses the alias 'Virginia' and was off our radar. She has no lease agreement, no official local address. Her ID is from Vermont. Not a fake though so she must have stolen it. We're trying to find the real Virginia now. Wouldn't be good if she came up missing, you know?"

"No, that would not be good." I paused a beat. "So, on a lighter

note, did you program my number into your phone? For the next time?"
I winked at her. Habit, possibly one I should break.

"What? For the next time you get abducted by some psycho chick?"

"Are you saying you're psycho too? Just my luck."

She giggled at that. Always have to keep the mood light, even in the most dire of circumstances.

"What's your first name, Officer Perez?"

"Linda."

"Linda. I like that. From the sound of it, you've been up all night."

"No big deal. You get used to it in this line of work. Adrenaline keeps you going."

"When is your shift over?"

"You're kidding, right? I mean, you're all cut up. You'll be in surgery--"

"Calm down. I'm just asking when your shift is over, nothing more. Just a citizen concerned for the well-being of an officer of the law. You need your rest."

She blushed. "I'm sorry. It just sounded like a come on."

"It was. But no worries. I'm sure I'll have to be around your neck of the woods for one thing or another with Ginny and all that. How about we meet up sometime soon, when you're not in uniform."

"Not in uniform?" She smiled devilishly. "You got it."

Turns out Ginny had in fact cut up that poor Dave Richardson guy. They found him in pieces locked in a freezer in the basement of the duplex. Luckily I don't think I need to be a witness in those proceedings since Ginny confessed. Not sure though. She still has a trial and all that. Still in the works. She confessed my ordeal as well. Not sure if they clump all these things together in one trial or separate. Just hoping I don't have to be too involved, any more than I already am. And the less I am personally related to it, the better.

I don't know what will happen to Ginny. I think she's wacko, she needs help. She also needs to be locked up, that's for sure.

As for me, I'm still in one piece thankfully. My ear was reattached and healed up quickly. My wrists and ankles are fine, only small slits that healed up neatly. My chest is different story. I'm scarred up, keloid. They're puffy so I now have the words "LOVER BOY' across my chest in uneven, angular scars. I've yet to take my shirt off in public, makes me look like I had it done on purpose. I guess I'll have to figure out what to tell the ladies about the scars. The only one who has seen them is my lady cop Linda. And yes, we're hot and heavy.

It's fitting though, the scars. For all things that are pleasurable in this life, there is an equal amount of pain. I've had my fair share of pleasure. Now I believe I've had my fare share of pain. And maybe I hurt Ginny in my own way, sure enough she thinks so. Maybe this lifestyle has hurt more girls than I realize. But I've brought happiness to a lot of girls too. There's the rub.

The doc says I can get the scars removed with lasers but it's not a guarantee that they won't come back. I've opted to just keep them. They act as a reminder to always consider the ladies on a deeper emotional level. Well, kind of. Mostly they act as a reminder to not get mixed up with any potential psycho chicks ever again.

THE END

Jason Salas has been producing his comic strip *Perk at Work* since late 2008. In 2014, he pulled the characters out of the panels and onto the page with these short stories. He plans on expanding the world of *Perk at Work* with more short stories and whatever else seems fun.

Jason Salas currently resides in Las Cruces, NM with his dogs Nugget and Babers, his pride and joy respectively.

www.ingramcontent.com/pod-product-compliance
Lightning Source LLC
Chambersburg PA
CBHW070644130626
46555CB00006B/2702